FLAMES *And* GUNSHOTS

Brinley Blake

Dedication

This book is dedicated to my family for their encouragement and support. It is also dedicated to all the young writers who share my enthusiasm for writing.

The publication of this book is proof that dreams really do come true.

Acknowledgement

I would like to acknowledge my Papa for helping to get my book published.

About The Author

Brinley Blake has aspired to be an author since a very young age. Born into a military family, she has lived in various US States before her family settled in CT. At the young age of 14, she completed her first book and is proud to present it to the world.

Table of Contents

Chapter 1:

The trees swayed whilst they disappeared behind me. I can't turn back. I hear the gunshots in the distance, even though we had only just discovered the horrors our lives would experience.

I had to run. I know if I survive, I'm most likely in trouble for the rest of my life, assuming my parents are still alive, but if I die, then there is a chance I would *still* be in trouble if I see my parents in the afterlife.

I need to hide. If anyone were to find me, anything could happen. I could even die. Cars are speeding somewhere, not sure where, but somewhere.

Car wrecks plague the center of town right now. One car had even crashed into the Town Hall.

I need to be sure of my safety. I didn't think to grab any supplies, which was an incredibly stupid decision for me.

All I have that's even remotely smart are the black running shoes, black leggings, and blue t-shirt I'm wearing, so I can easily maneuver my way around and try to outrun anybody who wants to kill me.

I'll need to gather resources soon, but I need to find at least a place to set up a little base, one that no one, and I mean *no one,* can find.

I have to run, but I can't breathe. I slow down, but keep myself moving, and I might be paranoid, but I keep looking around to make sure no one's following me.

I pass the Town Hall, the wreck being worse than I had thought, and I shudder at the dead bodies within the crash.

Against my better judgment, I pick a couple of flowers from the grass, and I place the makeshift bouquet on the front part of the car in respect.

I then bow my head for about three seconds, sending a silent prayer for the dead family to be blessed in the next life.

I then bolted away, about to cry. I wasn't even religious, but I hoped that family was somewhere better.

I spotted a cluster of trees nearby. That could be a decent place to hide out until something happened.

It'd be better than dying at the hands of aggressive people. Or some soldiers, but only if they invaded, but if they did, I feel as though they probably wouldn't target a tiny town like Brooklyn, Connecticut.

If any soldiers, or literally anyone outside of Connecticut, found out about Brooklyn, they would call you crazy and say there's only one, that's in New York.

However, there is a Brooklyn, Connecticut, just Google it. It's in the eastern part of Connecticut, near Rhode Island.

I know I shouldn't go to Walmart, as there will be *many* people trying to take over the whole thing.

Maybe I can sneak in and take some supplies and food whilst everyone's distracted. I might die, but it may be my best shot at actually surviving out here.

I made my way towards Walmart, as I wasn't that far from it, which would be a bad thing, because if there was anyone aggressive near Walmart, they would be able to find me fast.

However, I wasn't going to let some overthinking drive me away from possible resources and supplies. It's a small town, so proximity to Walmart shouldn't matter.

Seeing Walmart in the distance, I suddenly had second thoughts, but I needed to be brave, and I kept walking, against my gut and my conscience.

I heard gunshots in the distance again, but as I got closer to the Walmart, I knew they weren't coming from where I was, which made me breathe easier.

But then again, what I could see was perhaps more terrifying. I saw nothing. No cars, no blood, no dead bodies, nothing. I shivered, as the lack of visible violence or life should be promising, but it might mean that danger was vaster than I would think. I advanced closer and closer to the imposing Walmart, hesitating to go in, but I needed supplies.

Which was better? Dying of starvation, dehydration, and possibly any sicknesses, or being shot and or beaten up by a bunch of people I don't even know?

I decided to go in, but if I were to get jumped, I would make sure to beg for my death to be quick and the least painful.

I know that if anything, I would have a very painful death that was slow, but it doesn't hurt to ask, right?

I had to push the doors open, but the inside was scarily quiet. And dark. The only light was from the doors, and nothing else.

I rushed to the nearest self-checkout, as I've seen lighters there. As I suspected, there were lighters, so I grabbed as many as I could and lit one.

I headed to an area to find some sort of backpack for supplies. I mean, I don't think money and laws matter here anymore, so I just took the least noticeable one I could see in the dim light of my lighter.

After I shoved the lighters in the backpack, my next stop at Walmart was the food aisles.

I climbed the shelves, making sure not to fall, and pushed cans into my backpack, and thankfully, there were enough to last me a while.

I then made my way to the sections with medicine and bandages, taking as much as I could fit in the backpack.

Suddenly, I heard a noise, and I quickly zipped up the backpack and dashed out of the Walmart, trying to rationalize where that noise came from.

It was probably just a mouse, as this place is abandoned, and mice and other critters like to be in abandoned places.

As I left, I cut my arm on something. I gasped and immediately covered my mouth. I couldn't let anybody know I was here.

I took out the bandages from my bag and wrapped them around my wound, hoping it wouldn't get infected.

I navigated myself to where the Town Hall was, at least, so there I could find my way to the tree cluster.

As I neared the Town Hall, I squinted, and clearly, the flower bouquet I had left was gone.

I ran over to see if it might have fallen off the car, but it was nowhere to be seen.

I shivered. Maybe I should get back to the tree cluster soon, as someone dangerous could be near.

The tree cluster was up ahead, and I desperately needed to get away from any place where I could be jumped and killed.

I hoisted the backpack in a secure part of a tree and climbed. I lay in the tree, and it dawned on me.

The world basically ended, or at least shut down temporarily for a while. My lighter in hand, I shut it off, making sure no fires were to burn me and the other trees down.

I glanced up, and the clouds covering the sky shot gray light through the leaves, and I hoped it wouldn't rain.

Just in case it *would* rain, I dashed to Walmart again, against my better judgment, and grabbed a tarp and some scissors.

I cut the tarp to make sure it would keep me and the backpack safe, and also small enough that no one could notice it.

The sky was almost pitch-black as I lay in the tree under the tarp. It *did* look fitting for the hell this world's beginning to live in.

Thankfully, I remembered to grab rope earlier, thankfully, and tied a knot I hoped wouldn't come loose around me, and then the other end to the tree so I didn't fall out whilst sleeping, made sure my long, dark brown hair wasn't going to get caught on anything, and I closed my eyes for the first time since hell had been unleashed on Earth.

***

I awoke to more distant gunshots. Were there so many people having shoot-offs?

Honestly, I didn't want to investigate, so instead, I stayed in the tree. Thankfully, the rope didn't break, and I didn't fall or almost fall.

I glanced at my backpack's contents, which looked the same as they had a few hours ago. However, I felt really well rested, but it looked as though it was about eleven a.m.

I glanced at the sky from underneath the tarp and realized it must have been a whole day since I fell asleep.

I rubbed my eyes, hoping it was an illusion, but there wasn't anything that could have made me hallucinate.

I jumped off the tree with a can of tomato soup after untying the rope. I needed to cook the soup, but I didn't have much to cook it with.

I *did,* however, have a bunch of lighters, so I gathered some twigs from the ground and surrounded the pile with some stones to make sure I didn't start a forest fire.

The fire I lit was so beautiful. I didn't have any words. I then made sure not to burn myself as I warmed the soup can above the fire as if I were roasting marshmallows.

After about three minutes, I grabbed the can opener I had snatched my first time in Walmart, which was most likely yesterday, and managed not to spill much soup.

It took me about 2 minutes to finish the tomato soup, which I assumed was a pretty good time, but no one could judge me now, so who did I need to impress?

I put out the fire, as I didn't need any smoke signals to allow anyone to find me, but I'm pretty sure *someone* saw it, and now I feel as though I should move my little encampment.

I didn't, though, because I didn't even know where else I would go. I continued to stay in my tree, hoping no one would come and take my supplies.

Or beat me up, and possibly kill me. I don't even know how long I would survive like this.

I just sat in the tree, and then I just started to cry, not like sobbing immensely like a whiny toddler, but a silent crying.

A quiet weeping over the state of this world. I know other people have it *way* worse, but I feel as though I could cry too, since no one was around, I think.

I knew that this would happen, too! It was inevitable, but I just wished that I had a reason not to worry about being killed.

This was only the beginning, too. However, I know it's only a matter of time before somebody finds me and probably kills me.

I feel helpless. I feel as though I can't do anything anymore. I feel as though nothing really *matters* anymore.

When I was younger, I thought I would have a normal life. Nothing like this. I thought I would have had a *better* life.

At least better than the memory haunting my brain for years on end.

7 Years Earlier

I was outside, playing with some other kids on the playground. We had been making a bunch of food for the local animals, like squirrels and birds.

But then, Max Richardson, a jerk who hated me for some reason, decided to be an asshole and invite everyone in the neighborhood except for me to his birthday party. At the same time, riding his rich-ass bicycle too. As everyone gathered at his house, I couldn't help but wish Max would just go away.

Right there, I had wished that Max would just suddenly stop being so mean, so that we could at least be not best friends, but not mortal enemies.

However, that didn't happen. What did happen was that everyone had a lot of fun whilst I was abandoned at the playground, with no one to hang out with.

No one to even share this lonely experience with. The more I sat there, behind the bars that kept me from falling off the structure, my hatred for Max grew. I had even started crying. A silent cry. I knew better than to be loud anyway. They even had a piñata too. I felt more and more hatred fill my heart as they all had the best time of their lives. No one had left the playground.

I started not to care until they lit a bonfire so they could roast marshmallows.

I must have fallen asleep or something because before I knew it, I had been teleported, and everyone was looking at a ball of fire.

I had lit a marshmallow on fire, and I was at the party! I blew out the marshmallow, and was handed some chocolate and graham crackers to make a s'more, which I did, and then I ate it.

But when I finished, I had cleaned my face, and then Max approached me.

"Two things:

One, you're only here because my mom said so. Two, you're not really here."

I was confused, but then I awoke back at the playground and rubbed my eyes.

The memory still haunts me, even though I had moved, but not before Max and his family moved to Pennsylvania.

I was still in the tree, and the sun was still shining. The tarp was still above me and the backpack, for protection in case it suddenly rains or something.

But then my mind went to thunderstorms. The biggest threat to me had revealed itself, but thankfully, I don't think it will happen for a while, and I'll be sure to have moved camps by then, right?

I remembered the night everyone in the neighborhood was in a thunderstorm, and our parents hadn't called us back in.

We couldn't just go back in on our own because we were children and didn't want to risk getting struck by lightning, so we instead planned out places to sleep and make sure we didn't die.

Trees surrounded us, so we made sure to stay away from them as lightning was a big enemy.

However, wood chips were on the ground, and we needed shelter in the playground's equipment.

We had decided to sleep in the tube slide, which was huge, but then we saw lightning strike the nearby bay.

We screamed and immediately took our places in the tube slide, hoping for our survival through the night at least.

However, after about thirty minutes of us being outside, our parents started calling us in, which made us sigh in relief.

I lay in the tree, under the tarp, with a backpack, and shedding tears at my past and how I wished things could have been different, and wishing I could change the past.

I knew nothing would have stopped this, though. This damn hell was inevitable. There was nothing anyone could have done to stop this.

I decided to deal with thunderstorms and random shit later. I tied myself to the tree again and lay on the tree as the haunting memories of my past grasped onto me, keeping me from escaping.

Chapter 2:

I had awoken to more gunshots again. I believe there may be some sort of pattern happening, but then again, it could just be some dumb coincidence.

Thankfully, I was more certain of my plan to tie myself to a tree every time I slept, because it hadn't broken or anything.

I looked around, hoping no one was there. For a brief second, though, I thought I saw someone. Someone incredibly familiar. I looked around again for a second, but my eyes were then fixated on the boy standing on the ground, staring at me with concerned eyes.

His blonde hair slightly blowing in the wind, and his concerned eyes, which were a calming silvery blue, gazed at me and my little base on the tree branches, as though he were impressed with it.

I screamed. But, to not attract any more attention than I probably already had, I covered my mouth, which was still making scared noises.

"It's alright. I'm not gonna kill you." Dimitri Raymond said.

There was something calming about his voice. Something that softened my expression. "Okay. Why are you here?" I asked, trying not to sound rude, even though I probably did. "I need allies. You were the first that came into my dumbass mind." Dimitri slightly blushed, which set off all the signals in my brain that were telling me to tell him.

I had also slightly blushed, too, in response to seeing him blush, which I felt was too complicated to tell anyone, so I kept the strange phenomenon to myself.

"Well, damn, I never thought to look for allies," I muttered, almost embarrassed.

"Oh, I had just thought you didn't trust anyone."

"I don't," I responded bluntly, on instinct, too. "Well, you have a smart shelter, but aren't you aware of possible thunderstorms?" Dimitri commented, amused.

"I *did,* for your information, but I don't need to cross that bridge right now, do I?" I glared at the boy, who was still beaming from ear to ear. "Well, let's find a safer shelter, then!" Dimitri suggested, whilst I gave him a suspicious look.

"And you're not planning on killing me for supplies, are you?" I gave him a more intense look, hoping he would speak the truth.

"Of course not! Why would I want *your* supplies when I clearly have my own supply?" Dimitri showed me his supplies, which were in a heavy-duty backpack similar to mine.

"Alright, I'll trust you, but if this is some sort of trick-"

"It's not. I swear on my life."

Dimitri stuck out a hand for a truce, and I shook it, seeing as his hands were clearly not behind his back and not crossing his fingers.

The two of us agreed that we would share both of our arsenals of supplies and weapons to make sure we both survive.

Walking through the abandoned, desolate streets, I felt as though we were being watched, but I ignored all of my instincts, marking them as paranoia, since I was in the presence of someone else who had been surviving these past few days.

I didn't know where we were going, but I saw the school, so I assumed we were going there, or we were going somewhere near there. "I just need to grab something from the school real quick, so can you make sure all of our stuff stays safe?" Dimitri asked me.

I nodded, and he disappeared within seconds. I hadn't seen anyone following us, or anyone outside, for that matter.

Dimitri was the only person I had seen who was alive, at least.

I hoped no one would be here, so that Dimitri and I could just travel safely. I then had second thoughts about hanging with Dimitri, who was still in the school, and it had been about five minutes.

He was either having a hard time finding whatever he was trying to find, had been killed, or had been taken by some rogue group of sixth graders or something.

Or the worst possible outcome of them all. He could have been taken by a group of kids from our own grade and murdered in cold blood, because, knowing them, they would do that.

I continued to wait, hoping Dimitri would return safely. The sun was beginning to set in the center of the sky, and I had realized it had been hours.

I glanced around, wishing no one was there, and wanted to go look for him, but my body wasn't allowing me to.

All I could do was wait with the supplies. After what seemed like forever, I heard the doors open.

I prayed it was Dimitri, and not some crazy ass person that would kill me. "Hey, sorry it took me forever, but I finally found that secret pocket knife I had in my locker. Took a millennium to open it, though." "Do you even know what a 'millennium' is?" I asked, not convinced he actually knew what it was.

"Yes..?" He said, not convincingly.

"Oh my god, you know that I know that you're not smart!" I accused.

"Well, for your information, Miss I-Know-Everything, I know it from a book!" He scoffed, trying not to laugh, but failing miserably.

"Let's go." I snickered as I handed Dimitri his supplies.

"Thank you, Mrs. Raymond." He smirked at me as I blushed.

"Oh my god, I *hate* you! Plus, it's Livia Everett!" I mustered without laughing, but then I broke down into giggles as he continued to smirk like Flynn Ryder from Tangled.

I don't even know how he was even able to recreate the face, but he even made it more hilarious!

We continued to journey through what used to be a somewhat peaceful town in Connecticut, but now, it was reduced to just distant gunshots and the wind whistling. We made it to the intersection. Straight was where Delilah Mortimer's house was, right was where Walmart and many other buildings were, and left was one of the many ways to get back to my house.

We decided to go left, as that was also where the Town Hall was. I stared in the open fields, where I used to wish to run barefoot with the love of my life.

I keep telling myself to confess to him, because he keeps showing the signs he loves me too, but I still keep my love for him secret. At least as secret as I *can*.

We continued down the road, which would be incredibly dangerous for us, but with no cars around, we could walk on the road freely.

The sun illuminated my pale skin, like some other kids, like Isaac Morrigan, and even Dimitri.

I wondered if Isaac was even alive. Knowing him, he probably locked himself in a basement with all the cans of beans, corn, and soup in his house.

He probably died a day ago, or even two days ago, but who knows.

Dimitri and I stopped at the Town Hall, where the car lies, with the dead bodies of a family inside.

We nodded in remorse and then continued our journey to a safe shelter.

***

We've been unsuccessful in our pursuit of a reliable shelter to keep us and our supplies safe, so as we search, we've been crashing in the Town Hall.

I've been trying to keep track of how many days it's been, and I believe we're now on day ten.

In the morning, gunshots were still heard in the distance, and the car, with the dead family, was still stuck in the wall. We picked some flowers and set them on the roof of the car.

Afterwards, we tried going down the path towards the school, but stopped at the Post Office, which had a statue of Israel Putnam.

I gazed at the man on the horse, wondering what he would think of today and all the chaos.

Dimitri and I continued to search for a reliable shelter in the area, and I wondered if the church/daycare was a good place, but I decided against it, as it was probably controlled by weirdos by now or something.

The Post Office wasn't reliable, as most of the place was rotting packages and letters that would never be transported where they needed to go.

I decided to visit Israel Putnam's statue again, and I hope that I could have some sort of intuition, or whatever shit I needed, to find the perfect place to settle with Dimitri to ensure the safety of not just our supplies, but also ourselves.

I was still convinced that Dimitri could be pranking me, but recently, I've been having fewer and fewer of those thoughts.

"Hey…I think I have an idea." Dimitri approached me as he spoke.

"Yeah, what is it?" I asked, standing up from where I was crouching.

"I think we might be able to go to one of the neighborhoods near the school?"

"Sure, let's do that." I breathed. I had never been to any road near the school, but if Dimitri trusted it, I guess I could, as it's been a week, and nothing bad has happened yet.

We started to make our way to the road where our school was.

The road we agreed on was significantly close, but far enough that if we ever dared to venture back to the school, and a bunch of rogue kids chased us, we could hide here. I wondered if anyone had come here, and we were going to get jumped. I started trembling, but made sure to keep it hidden from Dimitri at least.

I couldn't ruin any chances of him actually liking me. For some reason, I feel as though he wouldn't like me if he learnt of my paranoia.

We walked the street, which was eerily quiet, except for the whistling of the wind, which added to the creepy aura.

I shuddered, and sadly, Dimitri noticed, and I felt incredibly guilty.

"I'm sorry! I'm not like, scared or anything, just still not really used to how quiet things are yet and-"

"No, no, it's okay if you're scared. I am too…" Dimitri smiled wryly as he spoke.

I smiled and felt as though my face had become a cherry. My eyes widened when he stared at me, and I slightly snickered while blushing as well.

"So, me turning into a cherry's funny?" I accused while laughing.

"Yeah, what of it, Everett?" He smirked.

"Well, I don't know…" I looked down, giggling. "I don't think it's embarrassing if that's what you think." Dimitri placed his warm hand on my shoulder, and I smiled meekly at him, still obviously blushing.

The two of us continued down the road, laughing and joking around, until we reached a quaint house, which Dimitri stopped at.

"You good, Dimitri?" I asked, concerned.

"Yeah, I just never thought my house would give me the creeps like this." Dimitri continued staring into the windows.

I glanced into the windows from the road, hoping no one was watching them. Thankfully, I couldn't see anyone, and before I knew it, we were continuing down the road. I didn't know if we needed to be at a certain house or something, and I just kept wondering if Dimitri had really thought this plan out thoroughly.

What if there were people? We couldn't really be sure, but there's always the chance, which was as terrifying as the fact that we could be completely alone right now.

We turned towards an area with some trees surrounding a clearing and set our supplies down.

The clearing was pretty secluded from the other roads, but if we weren't careful, people could potentially see us.

A house nearby, which had a pool, was the only thing that people could have in order to checkmate us.

"Hey, I'm gonna see if there's anything useful in that house," I informed Dimitri, who then nodded.

I advanced to the house, and checked the door and literally everywhere in case there were any traps set.

Thankfully, there weren't, so I opened the door, which was unlocked for some reason. The house was kind of dark, but the windows helped with that in addition to my lighter.

I checked every closet until I found a tent. A good size for both Dimitri and me, so I grabbed it and dashed out because I didn't like the vibes of that house.

"Hey, Dimitri, I found a tent!" I was out of breath, as the tent was kind of heavy, but I managed to start breathing at a regular pace. "Cool. We can use the trees to hang the tarp, protecting us from the rain!"

The two of us spent the next few hours trying to set up the tarp, which proved to be more difficult than we had anticipated. "Why did we think this would be a good idea?" I asked Dimitri in a joking manner, to which he started laughing.

"I don't know. I thought it would have been easier, honestly…" Dimitri trailed off, suddenly concerned about something behind me. "What's wrong?" I asked. I then immediately regretted asking when I heard a blade being unsheathed.

"Well, looks as though we have some youngsters in our territory…" A sharp male voice spoke behind me, with what was probably a fake New York accent.

I turned, and three men, around 20, maybe a little older, wearing the same clothes around one arm.

The insignia of a crown, with demon horns poking out, as well as all three wearing sleeveless shirts, showing off their obvious muscles.

My eyes widened and filled with tears. This was what I had feared. Now, it was reality.

Chapter 3:

I couldn't feel myself. I kept wishing that this was a dream, but I knew it was definitely real.

I wanted to fight, but the members of the gang were double my size and obviously stronger than me.

I looked at Dimitri and back at the gang. My eyes overflowed with fear, and I hoped the gang would leave us alone, but they had the advantage available to do whatever they pleased with us.

They were probably going to kill us. I didn't *want* to die, but if anything, I knew that they wouldn't kill us quickly and give us the least painful death, which was what I would personally want.

But instead, they would probably keep us somewhere and give us the slowest, most painful death ever, just for their own amusement.

I hate people. They're sick and have no motivation for the sick things they do. They have no morals and act like wild pack animals that prey on the smaller and/or weaker kind.

The gang was whispering to each other and glaring at us as we were frozen with horror. Suddenly, one of the gang members fell over. Behind him, a familiar girl held a bloody knife and smirked at the body in front of her.

"Hey! Hands up now!" The other gang members pulled out guns and pointed them at the girl.

I was staring at the body in fright. His blood was staining the grass, and the malicious cut was dark and starting to attract some bugs. I felt someone pull on my wrist, and I was moving somewhere, but still staring at the body.

A wave of darkness covered my eyes in an ocean of disturbance, and all I could hear was a faint, high-pitched buzzing that got louder by the second.

***

"Hey, Livia, wake up. We're safe." Dimitri's soft and faint voice spoke to me.

"But he was dead," I mumbled. It was blurry, but I could tell I was in some room or something.

"You're okay. I'm okay. You know Delilah Mortimer and Isaac Morrigan? They're here too. And that dude in the grade above us. Gabriel Leonardo? His younger sister Julia is here too." Dimitri mentioned.

I sat up, realizing I was in someone's house. I couldn't recognize whose house it was, though.

"Where are we?" I asked.

"My house," Delilah responded, caressing her knife darkly in the corner of her room. The shadows cast on her face made her icy blue eyes seem to glow. Her golden hair was cut shorter than I had last seen it. It looked a little disheveled, and her tan skin was darker in the low light.

"Here. Eat this." Delilah handed me a warm can of corn and a spoon.

As I ate the corn, Dimitri explained what had happened before I blacked out.

"So basically, Delilah and Gabriel were hunting for supplies there too, and they noticed we were cornered by the Kings of Hell, a self-proclaimed gang. Delilah was feeling a little feisty today, so she decided to sneak up and kill one, which would grab the attention of the other two, giving us a chance to escape, and Gabriel could kill the other two."

"Yeah, pretty much." Delilah nodded.

I finished half of the corn and set it down, wanting to ask a question.

"So, are the bodies just lying in the grass, or did something happen?" I had an idea of an answer, but hoped it wasn't true.

"Oh, yeah, we just nail the bodies to random trees, and make a message with blood, something like 'We're onto you,' or something creepy like that."

I shivered. I was thankful I hadn't seen any of those bodies, but I was even more thankful *I* wasn't one of those bodies.

"So, Isaac's here, too?" I asked.

"Yeah," Dimitri responded.

I stood up, careful not to fall over, and tried to find Isaac.

The pale, skinny, brown haired boy with bright hazel eyes was sitting on the couch, playing a video game.

His parents were pretty strict about video games, so I couldn't blame him for being completely focused on it.

"Oh! Livia! You're awake!" Isaac greeted me with a smile.

He set down the controller and came over to me. He used to be shorter than me, but I guess he gained some height since the last time I saw him.

"Hey, Isaac!" I greeted him. "Thought you'd be dead, honestly." I laughed awkwardly, but was happy when he laughed too.

"No, not dead yet, but I think I'm close. I don't think Delilah's quite fond of me." He muttered in a joking manner. Dimitri, Isaac, and I all laughed.

A taller boy entered the house, holding the body of a deer, and stared at me. He was incredibly ripped. Intimidated, I backed up a little bit.

He had sun-kissed skin and dark brown hair covering a little bit of his eyes. He had a scowl on his face, and it seemed permanent. "Um, I guess you're Gabriel?" I asked, hoping he was friendly, but I doubted it.

"Yeah…. I guess." He muttered, his chocolate-colored eyes not meeting my gaze, but that was alright. He seemed like a loner anyway. "He does that to everyone, including Delilah. Don't think Delilah likes it, though. But, then again, I don't think Delilah likes *anything* or *anyone*." Isaac informed me.

That was strange, since she always seemed close to me during school, even though we didn't have many classes together.

Gabriel trudged through the entrance and set the deer on the table. A speck of blood flung onto his white shirt, but he didn't seem to care.

Dirt covered the bottom of his black boots, and there was a little mud on his camouflage pants.

"I got dinner tonight! Gonna roast it outside now!" I assumed Gabriel was yelling to Delilah, who was still in the other room.

"Ok!" A faint yell from Delilah answered.

Gabriel picked up the deer's body again and walked out the back door. A small and thin girl, probably ten, walked into the living room and sat herself on the couch.

She had a white shirt on, with some dirt on it, and black shorts. She had a Band-Aid on her right leg, pristine. *Probably a recent injury,* I thought.

"I assume you must be Julia Leonardo?

Gabriel's younger sister?"

"Oh, are you Livia? Everyone says good things about you. Yes. I'm Julia Lorelei-Leonardo, but I'm not that much younger than Gabriel. I'm twelve now. Just a year or two younger than you guys, I think."

Everyone nodded, and I felt somewhat bad for Julia. She legitimately looked like she was ten years old.

Julia shrugged and lay her head on a black sweatshirt next to her.

"Whose sweatshirt's that? It's cute." I asked, wanting to keep a conversation going, so I didn't feel awkward.

"Oh, I think it's Gabriel's. I like to steal it. Just don't tell him. I honestly never have a clear answer on how he would react to certain things, but I have some ideas…." Julia trailed off as she fell asleep.

I carefully placed myself on the couch, and Dimitri sat right next to me, making me feel sick to my stomach. I didn't know how to respond.

Dimitri put his arm around my shoulders, and out of instinct, I placed my head on his shoulder. It felt amazing. I've never done it before, and I didn't realize how *right* it felt.

I smiled, feeling warm and somewhat numb, and didn't want this to end.

***

Gabriel returned to Delilah's house, carrying a cooked deer.

"Dinner's ready!" Gabriel boomed, rolling his eyes.

The deer was placed on the table, and several plates and silverware were in front of the six chairs.

Gabriel sat at one end of the table, Julia next to Gabriel, and Isaac next to Julia. I sat as far away from Gabriel as I could, and Dimitri sat between Gabriel and me.

Delilah entered the dining room, her blade in her bun. I stared, but only for a second, as I didn't want her to think badly of me.

Delilah sat next to me, at the opposing end of the table.

"Tradition Time," Gabriel muttered to everyone.

Gabriel gently held Julia's hand, who held Isaac's hand, who held Delilah's hand.

Gabriel and Delilah gestured for Dimitri and me to hold each other's hands, and their hands too.

"Lord, if you even exist, please let this venison nourish our bodies so we can survive the hell that has burdened this Earth. Please keep us safe from the dangers of this new world. Amen."

"Amen." We responded in unison.

Gabriel took a large knife and cut some of the venison, and handed the meat to Julia. As Gabriel handed pieces of meat to everyone, I was confused about what the point of that was.

I'm not religious, but my dad and his side of the family are, and they never said anything like that.

I decided to stop pondering when Dimitri placed the venison Gabriel gave to him to give to me on my plate.

When everyone was served, we started eating the deer. As we ate, I kept wondering why Delilah and Gabriel saved us. The subject was then interrupted by Delilah, who decided to start a conversation. "So, what do you people think happened to the teachers?" Delilah said while taking another bite of venison.

"Personally, I think Mr. Kreefir *could* have survived, but when it comes to Mr. Popidip, I *hope* that jack-ass died!" Isaac exclaimed.

"Honestly, you know who probably *did* survive? Ms. Zeega!" I responded.

Everyone nodded, except for Julia and Gabriel. I assumed Julia didn't because she didn't know who Ms. Zeega was, which was understandable, but when it came to Gabriel, I just assumed he didn't want to talk about this shit.

Most of us just ate, laughed, and talked shit about pretty much everyone we knew, except Gabriel, who finished his venison and just went to a room, which I assumed was his room here.

When we finished, Delilah showed me where she and Julia slept.

I learned that the girls, as in Delilah, Julia, and now, myself, slept in Delilah's room, which had a lot of blankets and pillows.

The boys slept in the room where Gabriel had disappeared earlier.

Delilah handed me a pair of pajamas from her dresser, and I put them on, as Julia finished putting on an oversized shirt and some shorts, which looked quite hilarious on her, but I didn't comment or laugh.

We all lay in the mess of blankets and pillows, and I passed out as soon as my head hit a pillow.

Suddenly, I was in a forest, running for my life, and I glanced behind me, and the body of Julia was in my arms, as Isaac and I carried her, but then, the two disappeared, and I was in the dirt, surrounded by fire.

But then, I saw someone. I saw a figure, who looked female, and a body beside her, and she was smiling.

Not happy, but insanely. Almost inhuman. I was terrified. I didn't even know what was happening.

I then heard a gunshot, and she was still smiling as she fell into the dirt of the forest. I was dragged away.

I awoke in the dim lighting of LED light strips along the walls of Delilah's room.

That *had* to be fake, right? That couldn't have been real. It *couldn't be.*

My head fell back onto a pillow, and I was transported somewhere else.

I was in the room, and I saw Delilah and Julia sleeping. However, I also saw myself sleeping.

Upon further inspection, I realized it was me! For some reason, I didn't feel much confusion, so I just decided to explore the house.

The house was pretty dark, but I switched the light on, and no one woke up, so I just walked through the house.

I went to where I thought was Delilah's parents' room, and realized it was, because no one was in it.

I knew it could be considered wrong, and maybe even illegal, but for one, my body's in Delilah's room, and two, the law doesn't even matter anymore, I don't think.

I then decided to snoop through the room a little, and ended up finding a lot of clothes, shoes, and random stuff.

I wondered what happened to Delilah's parents. *Did they die?*

I didn't know the answer, but what I *did* know was that I should probably go back to my body and actually have a more normal dream instead of this strange phenomenon.

I made my way back to Delilah's room again and tried to get back into my body.

Eventually, I phased back into my body and then woke up again. It was probably about four in the morning, but I didn't check the alarm clock.

I fell back asleep again, wanting a more normal dream, like flying on a Pegasus or something stupid like that.

Thankfully, I ended up on a beach, watching the waves wash upon the shore, and the sun setting below the waters.

I looked beside me, as there was an arm around my shoulders, holding me close. Turns out, it was Dimitri.

I didn't even question it. I liked it. Wait, no, I *loved* it. *A lot,* in fact. I just sat with Dimitri, a peaceful evening, just us, together.

Dimitri smiled at me. His eyes were beautiful gems. Pale blue-gray gems, sparkling at me.

I smiled back, wanting, but continuing to hesitate, but then, I remembered there wasn't anyone around.

I leaned in and had my first-ever *true* kiss with Dimitri Raymond.

May

June

Chapter 4:

"Breakfast!"

I heard Gabriel's still uninterested voice boom through the fantasies, and I was back in Brooklyn, Connecticut, with a group of kids that I sometimes wonder if they'd willingly sacrifice me to soldiers if they had the chance.

I groggily made my way to the dining room. Everyone except Delilah was sitting at the table.

She was probably going to the bathroom or something.

"Was there a tornado in the girls' room last night?" Dimitri jokingly poked at me and Julia's hair, which was incredibly messy. "All I know is that Delilah's gonna criticize us when she sees us," I responded. Julia nodded in agreement.

Gabriel brought out some berries and pancakes.

"Is it safe?" Dimitri asked.

"Yes, my parents always put the pancake mixer in the freezer to last longer in case we forget about it." Delilah walked in, hair brushed. "You two have a rat's nest for hair, and I can't even deal with *you three!*"

Dimitri and the boys grinned at her, who was visibly annoyed at their antics. I shrank in my seat.

"Tradition Time...I guess." Gabriel sat in his chair, taking Dimitri's and Julia's hands as the rest of us took hands.

"Lord, if you're not ignoring our cries, please bless the food we are about to eat with the strength to continue through this terrifying time," I noticed Gabriel getting more and more physically annoyed, "and please bless this food so we can be protected from any danger. Amen."

"Amen."

As we took pancakes and berries, I thought I sensed people judging me, so I only took one pancake.

Part of my brain thinks no one was judging me, which I think people would call that part the "sensible one."

I made sure to take a small amount of berries too, so that I don't seem fat. I think I already *am* fat, even though people say I'm not.

I'm not sure what to believe, but whenever I eat, I make sure to make myself not look as fat as I feel.

"So, what are we gonna do today?" Isaac asked with a mouthful of his pancake, which made me almost gag up my pancake.

"We don't need to stock up on food, cause of soup, but we do need to get some weapons for these two." Gabriel pointed to Dimitri and me. "What? Is my pocket knife not good enough?" Dimitri asked jokingly, stuffing his face with pancake.

I continued eating, hoping no one was judging me, which they probably were. I desperately didn't want to be killed by them, or anything like that.

We continued eating, and when we were all done, Gabriel grabbed Dimitri and me, and before I knew it, we had driven a truck from Delilah's house to an abandoned store.

Gabriel tossed a gun to me, and I barely caught it, making sure I didn't shoot anything or anyone.

Thankfully, I didn't, but Gabriel shook his head and took the gun back, placing it back on a shelf.

Dimitri walked to me with a gun strapped to his back.

"Russian AK-47. My favorite." He had placed his hand on my shoulder and then handed me a similar gun.

"Assault rifle, you look like you have good aim," Gabriel muttered to me.

"Thanks…. I guess?" I didn't know how to respond.

Was it a compliment, or was it not? I had no idea, but I couldn't dwell on that.

The three of us then exited the store and hopped back into the ebony truck, which I was positive Gabriel stole, and drove about ten to fifteen minutes back to Delilah's house.

During the ride, Dimitri and I decided to be in the bed of the truck, and since there was technically no one to stop us, we were lying in the bed of the truck while Gabriel drove.

"You ever wonder what life would be like if none of this had happened?" I asked, staring at the cyan sky, the sun shining on my face.

I thought I was going to get a sunburn, but if I did, then surely Dimitri would too; we were both wearing similar clothing, and both have a tendency to burn easily.

"Hmm. I know, right?" Dimitri sighed, "I honestly think maybe we could have a normal life together?" He smirked at me, and I felt myself blushing and heating up.

"God. Why are you like this?" I stayed laying down next to him.

"I thought you weren't religious!" He smirked. "Whatever!" I laughed, not even hiding my smile.

He then decided to edge his hand closer and closer, and then hold my hand.

I didn't *hate* it. I actually loved it. A *lot,* in fact. I think I blushed again, because he snickered again, which would only make me blush more.

Eventually, I started falling asleep for some reason. Maybe it was because of a lack of sleep? No.

I decided to just go with whatever was happening. I felt Dimitri pull my body into his, and I buried my head into his shoulder. "I don't exactly hate this...." I mumbled as we snuggled, the slight bumps keeping me aware of the situation.

I couldn't explain it, but I want to do this forever, but I also wanted *not to do this*, but it was starting to be numbed by the thrill of this. I loved him. I loved Dimitri. I hadn't even told him, but I have a feeling he knows. I also think he knows that I have a feeling he has a crush on me, too.

But it could all be a terrible prank. My mind always goes to this whenever a positive thing goes through my mind.

I *hate* the fact that my mind does this, but sometimes I kind of believe some of the things it tells me could be true in some cases.

Now I remember why I haven't told Dimitri yet, because of my stupid negativity that plagues my mind.

How do I actually make it stop? Or at least keep it incredibly small, so that I can ignore it easily?

That question has been unanswered since I started trying to find a solution for it.

I have Googled how to keep it at a manageable level, but whenever I try a new solution, it always fails after about a week.

I have since then stopped trying. I don't think it's really worth it anymore.

For now, I am in the bed of an ebony truck with the love of my life, snuggling at about ten a.m. I loved this more than I could ever describe.

We pulled into Delilah's driveway, clouds starting to flow through the sky.

"S'it gonna rain? Damn." Dimitri asked Gabriel, who pulled out the guns from the truck.

"Better not," Gabriel muttered, handing us our respective weapons.

I was caught off guard when Dimitri scooped me from the truck bed and placed me onto the rocky driveway, where I almost fainted, but caught myself.

"Thanks!" I smiled at Dimitri, who then hopped out of the bed and smiled back. "If you two are done with your romance, can we actually go inside?" Gabriel gave us a dirty look as he spoke.

We were ushered inside, hoping not to draw any attention towards ourselves from anyone who could be dangerous.

"Look who's back!" Isaac called, I assumed to Julia, who then ran up to Gabriel, and the two hugged.

"Now that's something I've never seen," I commented to Dimitri, who nodded. "We got guns!" Dimitri informed Isaac and Delilah, who had just come out into the living room.

"Oh god," Delilah muttered, annoyed. I wondered what *her* problem was.

Dimitri showed Isaac his gun, and I just pondered on what Delilah had against Dimitri. *Wait,* I thought, *not my business.*

I showed my assault rifle to Isaac, who gazed at it with wide eyes.

"I only have a regular shotgun. Yours is *so* cool!" He smiled at me as he explained.

I heard thunder rumbling in the distance, which caused Julia to jump a little. "It's okay, Julia." Gabriel comforted, which confused me even more.

Why was he being so caring with Julia? He's usually so.... *not* like that towards anyone else since I've been here.

Malevolent clouds hovered in the sky, spreading across Brooklyn.

"Ooh! I have the *best* idea!" Julia announced with wide eyes. "How about we all change into comfortable clothes, turn down the lights, put on some dumb movies or something, and just chill."

Everyone yawned, not dismissing Julia's idea, but proving the importance.

"Yeah, I think we need to relax," Dimitri admitted.

With everyone agreeing, Julia ran to the pantry and put bags of popcorn in the microwave.

"You sure it's safe for us to use the microwave during a thunderstorm?" I asked, worried.

"Yeah, it's fine. I don't think we'll be electrocuted or something." Julia responded reassuringly.

Gabriel, Dimitri, and Isaac entered the boys' room and changed into comfortable clothes, then came back out and moved the furniture into positions to allow us to relax.

From there, Delilah led Julia and me to the girls' room, where we changed as well. "I think the popcorn will be done soon," Julia said, pulling her hair out from under her shirt. She left the room and scampered down the hall as Delilah and I finished getting dressed.

Delilah looked through her DVDs and pulled out Sleeping Beauty, Cinderella, The Emperor's New Groove, and Moana.

"Which one first?" Delilah asked us.

"Probably Moana." We said in unison.

We then stared at each other for a second, and then laughed uncontrollably. Eventually, Julia returned with popcorn, which was all separated into big bowls, and we partnered up with someone.

Julia and Gabriel were together, and Isaac and Delilah, who left Dimitri and me.

We all lay on the couch, snuggling with blankets, and singing all the Moana songs. "I love this." I whispered to Dimitri, who mumbled a slight "same."

As we sang the Moana songs, the sky darkened even more, which kept me on my toes, but I tried to relax.

We all continued to watch the movie and sing, but I think Gabriel fell asleep at some point.

"Y'know, I think this movie was the best when it came out," I murmured, on the verge of falling asleep against Dimitri's body. "I think it's because Lin-Manuel Miranda wrote the songs for the movie…he writes the best songs. I mean, In the Heights, Hamilton, etcetera." No one responded in words, which was fine.

I wondered if I should consider them friends. I mean, they *did* save Dimitri and me from being slaughtered by a gang, so perhaps I *should* consider them *friends.*

The sky only darkened more as time went on. Everything felt kinda hazy, and at times, I felt sort of dizzy, as though I were in a gyroscope, or if I were on a rollercoaster where you go in a loopy-loop.

My eyes closed, slowly encasing me in the darkness, the warmth of both the blanket and Dimitri's body guiding me into a trance. However, I couldn't fall into the trance. Or sleep. I was on the *verge* of a sleepy trance, but it was annoying, just being on the sweet, sweet verge of sleep, but I couldn't fall asleep.

I stayed in this, almost paralyzed in place, fearing the ability to move.

I think everyone else fell asleep, which made me envy them. Lucky them! They were able to sleep while I'm just on the verge.

It felt *really weird* to supposedly be the only one awake, but I ignored the creepiness of it all and just focused on the sound of the movie and not the harsh rains outside.

I remembered the times I've felt this *warm,* or just felt like I was *at home.*

It was an amazing feeling, an amazing sentiment, it was just overall the *greatest* feeling ever, and I'm still not sure how to word it.

I was still lying against Dimitri's body, which rose and fell with every breath he took, so I knew he was at least *alive.*

Suddenly, for some reason, my mind trailed off to an old video game from the past. School of Dragons. My childhood. Spent my days going to school, coming home to go on the laptop, and playing the game.

Quests, collecting dragons, flying, and exploring different maps, it was paradise.

I had only *just* gotten back into it when the game's fate was sealed. It was shut down forever at the end of June two years ago, and true to its word, you can't find it on the App Store anymore.

Strangely, the website and YouTube channel are still up, not *active,* but still reachable.

Finally, I think I'm able to fall asleep, and we're nearing the end of Moana right now, too!

I start to spin again, and the feeling of falling is present as well, which is a little strange, but it's better than being on the verge of sleep.

The darkness is enclosing around me, and I welcome sleep with open arms, feeling even more warmth.

I snuggle closer, and the sweet sensation of sleep hits me, creating a soft atmosphere where the sound of Moana is "drowned" out.

***

We awoke to darkness, which was because the power had shut off. It was about five a.m., and the sky was starting to clear up. I heard a noise. It was a tapping, and I jumped as I heard it.

"You alright?" Dimitri asked, glancing at me with concern in his beautiful eyes. I almost got distracted, but eventually, I managed to spit out a "yes."

"Just heard a noise, that's all." I clutched my gun closer to my chest, hoping nothing would snatch me into the darkness.

We all huddled closer together, tired and scared, the darkness taunting us as we hoped no one had broken in.

"Y'know, we should find a flashlight or something..." Gabriel whispered, no fear in his voice.

I remembered my lighter, which *should* be in my pocket, hopefully.

"I have my lighter!" I whisper-shouted in excitement.

"Good. Now go see what's making that noise." "What the hell?!" I shrieked in confusion.

I immediately regretted what I had done. My eyes widened, and I awaited to be shot, or stabbed, or literally anything bad to happen, but after a few seconds, nothing happened.

I held my breath still, almost passing out entirely, but nothing happened, and we were still huddling together.

"Ok, but you still need to be the one to check what it was." Delilah pressured.

My eyes were only getting wider, and my chest was thumping so hard, I thought my heart would just burst out of my chest.

Time seemed to slow, making everything worse.

"Why do *I* have to be the one?" I asked, hoping to get someone else to do it.

"Because *you* have the lighter, duh!" Delilah rolled her eyes at me, as though I were the dumbest person on the planet.

"But-"

"I don't wanna hear any excuses!" Delilah crossed her arms and narrowed her eyes at me. "But why her? If anything, it should be you, since you're so eager to send Livia out there." Julia fought, raising an eyebrow.

"Yeah! You shouldn't just sell me out!" I protested.

I wondered if she was trying to find a reason to get me killed. This was probably because I'm annoying, or maybe because she was bored, and she wanted to make things interesting or something.

I stared at her, who was just staring back, looking all "innocent." I narrowed my own eyes at her, feeling my anger and betrayal brewing up inside me, but I knew I shouldn't get too annoyed.

Julia, Gabriel, and Isaac gathered around Dimitri and me, whilst Delilah just stood on the other side of the room, holding her knife and still crossing her arms.

"Well, for one, your romance is *very* annoying, and two, I'll go check the noise."

Delilah stormed into the darkness, leaving the rest of us in the living room with the light of my lighter to guide us through the shadows.

"That seemed weird, didn't it?" Julia broke the silence.

We nodded in agreement, as it was, in fact, weird as hell.

After about five minutes, Delilah returned, holding a dead rat.

"Ew!" Julia shrieked, jumping back from Delilah.

"It's dead. That's what was making the noise. Killed it. There." She dropped it on the floor and then looked at us like we owed her something.

"What?" I asked.

"You gonna say thank you, or.."

"We don't owe you anything!" Dimitri yelled.

"Yeah! You tried to possibly get Livia killed!" Isaac accused, and we all nodded.

"Alright! Alright!" Delilah raised her arms in defeat.

"Apologize to Livia!" Gabriel told her.

"But-"

"*Apologize.*" Gabriel gave a warning look to Delilah.

"*Fine.* I apologize to you, Livia. For trying to 'get you possibly killed.' I hope you can forgive me." She gave *the most* sarcastic tone ever, but I took it anyway.

"I forgive you, Delilah," I responded, not smiling.

The sun was starting to rise, and Gabriel grabbed his gun.

"Gonna hunt. For dinner later. Someone can make breakfast if you want."

I made my way to the kitchen and searched the pantry for something for breakfast.

When I found something, I started making it, hoping that by the time Gabriel arrived back, it would be ready.

For some reason,I felt as though Delilah's knife was slowly descending into my back, but it wasn't physically.

I wondered what it meant, but I then dismissed it, thinking it was just overthinking.

I mean, it probably was. It always *is* just overthinking.

July

August

Chapter 5:

Gabriel and I have teamed up for cooking. He would hunt and gather food for dinner whilst I made breakfast.

This morning, I had just finished the rest of the French toast and scrambled eggs. Dimitri went to help Gabriel find a place to keep the fish fresh for dinner.

"Breakfast's ready!" I called.

Isaac and Julia rushed to the table, already smelling the French toast. Delilah followed, still visibly annoyed from being given an ultimatum, even though it had been a couple of months or so.

"French toast and scrambled eggs?" Julia asked excitedly.

Gabriel and Dimitri returned, sitting down and sniffing the warm aura of cinnamon. "Tradition Time…" Gabriel announced tiredly, as though he had stayed up all night, but was still surprisingly able to keep his uninterested demeanor.

As we held hands and closed our eyes, I wondered if this, or anything, meant anything to Gabriel and the others, but I had to instead focus on what Gabriel was saying.

"Lord, God, you're probably laughing at the destruction happening to our world, but past all of that, please bless the food we have received and are about to eat with protection from the dangers of this world today, and please have this end soon. Amen."

"Amen."

We began to eat, and the silence haunted me and taunted me at the same time.

I desperately wanted to break the silence, but I just couldn't.

"So, what's the plan for today?" Julia asked, a mouthful of scrambled eggs being exposed to all of us as she spoke.

I quietly sighed, feeling saved by the break in the silence.

"We should probably check around the house, make sure nothing was compromised, nothing broken," Delilah responded, setting her fork down.

"You know, I have a question, Gabriel…" I started, feeling his stare pinning me to the chair like a spear, "Why do we do the 'Tradition Time' when you don't seem to really care about it? Like, I'm not trying to insult you, or say that I care about it, I'm just saying-"

"Livia? Can you and I talk in the hallway *alone?*" Gabriel gritted his teeth as he spoke, which sent shivers down my back.

I carefully arose from the chair and followed Gabriel into the hall.

"Look. I'll just give you the simplest answer: For Julia's sake."

My brow rose. I was confused. I didn't believe it could be possible, but then I remembered the thunderstorm from two months ago, and everything that had transpired that night.

Gabriel had comforted Julia every time she was sad about something. I then realized how possible it actually *was.*

"Now, let's get back to breakfast." Gabriel trudged back to the dining room and sat back down.

I followed and continued eating, just thinking of why Gabriel was always doing stuff for Julia.

The two don't really look alike, so I don't think they were *siblings,* but maybe cousins? *Wait,* I thought, *I'm overthinking again. Focus on the food. Try to imagine what the process of digesting food looks like right now, as you're eating.* Or maybe I should play some music in my head? I have many options, and perhaps I can find a way to make art after breakfast!

I finished breakfast, and so did Isaac and Dimitri.

"Hey, do you have anything to draw with?" I asked Delilah.

"Yeah, check the drawers in the closet." Delilah pointed to her room.

I entered her room and resisted the urge to snoop too much.

After finding some paper and a pencil, with a good eraser too, I made my way to a flat surface to draw.

I never know what to draw, I just draw whatever comes into my head. Today, I guess what my head came up with was to draw random characters.

I don't know how much time passed, but I don't care either way. Julia came over and sat next to me.

"Hey, Julia!" I smiled at her, and she smiled back.

"What are you drawing?" Julia asked.

"I don't know, just some random characters."

"Well, they kinda look like Isaac, Dimitri, and Gabriel." She turned to the drawings, and that's when I noticed a nasty scar on her right cheek. "Where'd you get that from?" I asked her, pointing at the scar.

"Oh, Delilah accidentally got me with her knife. It's *really sharp.*"

Julia smiled weakly and laughed a little, but I was genuinely concerned for her.

Could Delilah do that to anyone? I immediately regretted the ultimatum from those months ago, since it looks like Delilah's holding a grudge now.

Julia and I sat there, staring at each other, and then, everything flashed before my eyes.

I heard screaming. I think it was Julia. The door was broken down, and men stormed into the house.

I didn't even know what was happening. We were running, but the men surrounded us.

Gabriel got into the truck, and Dimitri and Isaac got Julia and me into the truck, whilst Delilah fought through the men.

We sped away, guns shooting at us, so we kept our heads down and covered, making sure no glass hit us.

I don't even think we had seatbelts on, but that was fine, as I didn't really care.

I felt dizzy, my vision blurring, but I managed to keep consciousness, for some reason, and we continued to drive, Isaac repeatedly checking for anyone following us, and I don't think anyone was, which was good for us.

"So, where do we go now? We don't have our supplies!" Isaac bit his fingernails, sweating intensely.

"First, we go find some more supplies, and then, we go into the woods. Near the school." We all stared at Gabriel as though he were insane.

"That's a terrible plan! We don't know if Walmart is overrun with these soldiers, and the woods are perilous!" Delilah reprimanded him.

"Which is why we should do this! It might still have some supplies! Especially since the gas won't last forever!" Gabriel argued.

Tears were running down my face as I held Julia close. I'm not sure if she was crying too, but either way, what just happened was shocking.

Gabriel pulled over at Walmart, and we split up. Isaac, Julia, and I stayed to guard the truck while Dimitri, Gabriel, and Delilah investigated and robbed Walmart. As Dimitri, Gabriel, and Delilah were in Walmart, probably being killed or something, Isaac, Julia, and I focused on keeping the truck safe.

"So, are we just gonna ignore the fact that the others could be dead in there?" I blurted, and then covered my mouth, my eyes widening with fear.

"Well, here's the thing," Isaac explained, "they *can't* be dead because there were vehicles at Delilah's house, but none here, so I'd say all of us are safe."

"For now…" I muttered, still thinking there was still a chance they could be dead.

I worried about the others. Well, mostly Dimitri, but definitely Gabriel, and I have no idea about Delilah.

The sun continued to rise, somewhat taunting us as the temperature only got higher.

We continued to sit in the truck, sweat dripping down our faces and necks.

I was tempted to turn on the air conditioning, but I couldn't move. It reminded me of sleep paralysis, but I was awake. "When do you guys think they'll be back?" I asked, feeling awkward sitting in silence, just sweating.

"I honestly have no idea. Are they taking their sweet time there or something?" Isaac responded, gesturing to the absurdity of the time taken.

Silence fell over us again, not because of the intense heat or anything like that, but because we heard gunshots in the distance.

We hid in between the front seats and the back seats, hoping no one could see us through the window.

The truck is really tall, so someone about seven feet tall *should* be able to spot us, but we don't know anyone that height, so we should be good.

I could hear muffled voices outside the truck. I think they were trying to hide or something.

I peeked through a puncture hole from one of the gunshots from the soldiers.

There were two people, both of them girls. I could recognize them, too.

"Are you *sure* those soldiers didn't follow us?" Alli Divas asked nervously.

"I'm sure. We need to get supplies." Molly Omitterres responded.

"Was going to Sophia Saonn's house and…you know… is *it* worth it? The soldiers found us, and the noise, so was it?" Alli whispered in an anxious tone.

"I'd say yeah, cause I'm pretty sure we don't have to deal with *her* again, so yeah," Molly announced proudly.

What happened to Sophia Saonn? Did she die? I mean, I don't exactly *care* if she *had* been killed by soldiers, as she's very annoying. I don't blame Molly and Alli for what they could have possibly done at Sophia's house, but I kinda wanna know what exactly they did.

Does this mean that others from our grade are surviving? Like Avery Marengo, or Kira Zapazil?

"I don't know why, but I kinda feel as though we're being watched…" Alli shivered whilst looking around.

When she turned to the truck, towards me, my face turned pale, and my eyes widened. I knew she couldn't possibly see my eye watching them through the bullet hole, because it was very small, but something just scared me.

"I wonder if that truck's owned by someone," Alli muttered while admiring it from the bush next to the girls.

Please don't notice me…Please don't notice me… I have *never* wanted to be noticed by the kids in my grade.

For one, they were incredibly insane and outlandish, and second, I've had a fair share of negative experiences with *these* particular girls.

I continued to watch as the girls inspected the truck outside.

I was shaking, which didn't help me, but thankfully, they couldn't see us through the window, which saved us.

"Hey, Livia?" Julia whispered, sounding scared. "Yeah?" I whispered back, hoping the girls didn't hear me. "Who's outside?"

"Some girls from school," I responded, trying to sound calm, but my shaking didn't help me out.

"What's wrong? Why're you shaking?" Julia kept her voice quiet, and I don't think the girls could hear us.

"They don't have weapons, and they don't have good combat skills, but somehow, I'm still scared of them. I think they lost their supplies too, trying to escape soldiers."

Julia held me close as I returned to peeking at the girls' activities through the bullet hole, hoping they wouldn't notice.

The girls continued to inspect the truck, looking closely at the details of the bullet holes, but when they went to the hole I was peeking out of, I just covered it with a random dark scarf I found on the truck's floor.

I think it worked because I could hear them walking away from the bullet hole after about 2 seconds of peeking through on the outside.

The girls eventually shrugged and tried tugging on the doors, trying to open them, but thankfully, we had locked the doors when Gabriel and the others left for Walmart.

"They're trying to get in…" I whispered to the other two, hoping to get some feedback on how to keep them from eventually finding a way to break in.

"I don't know what to do!" Isaac whisper-shouted, while still keeping at a volume the girls wouldn't hear.

"Well, should we just let them try to break in?" I asked, even more sweat dripping down my face than before.

It was a desert in the truck right now, and the girls trying to break in were making everything way worse than before.

"What happens when they break in?" I asked, already knowing a couple of answers.

"I mean, they don't really pose a threat, but we don't have any weapons either, so we might not have much of an advantage over them, unless any of you have secret hand-to-hand combat skills?" Isaac responded, trying to be helpful, but honestly, it wasn't that helpful.

"That wasn't that helpful, no offense, but we should definitely try to fight if they break in," Julia told Isaac, who then hung his head in shame, but then brought it back up.

We continued in the dance of the girls trying to break in, and us, in a stalemate.

None of us had an idea of what to do. All we could do was hope that either the girls would give up trying to break in, which wasn't going to happen, sadly, or that Gabriel, Dimitri, and Delilah would return from Walmart.

Suddenly, the loudest gunshots I ever heard were fired, and I took a look outside the bullet hole, and Molly and Alli were on the ground, dead.

Chapter 6:

"What the hell just happened?" Isaac whispered, his eyes the size of oranges.

"Someone shot them…" I whispered back, my voice cracking a couple of times as well.

I didn't know who was responsible, but I hoped and prayed it wasn't a soldier or a posse of soldiers.

There was a tug on the doors to the driver's seat, and I made my way to a position so I could try to spot who was trying to get in. I could see dark brown hair, which made me think of Gabriel, but I could be wrong.

The tugging continued, and I could hear muffled voices outside. This time, they were on Isaac's side.

"Could you try to distinguish whose voices they are?" I whispered to Isaac, clearly terrified of the possible threats outside.

"Ok." He responded, putting his head against the door, his eyes widening.

"What? Who is it?" I asked, getting a little louder.

"It's Gabriel, Dimitri, and Delilah." He sighed in relief.

I went to unlock the doors, and when they did, the others opened the doors with brute force and gave us a dirty look as we looked at them, still a little shaken.

"Okay, just because two girls come looking at this truck and get shot, doesn't mean you can't recognize us from where you guys were!" Delilah reprimanded, which seemed a little unnecessary, but I didn't need to be in an argument with her again.

The others hopped into the truck, giving us some of the supplies to carry, and we sped off from Walmart.

When we turned down the road to the school from the Town Hall, Delilah started to get irritated for some reason.

"Why do we need to go to the woods? Especially the ones near the school?" She gave a disapproving look to Gabriel, who just sighed and rolled his eyes.

He pulled over, hiding us near the bushes, and turned towards the rest of us.

"So, since Delilah thinks the woods are a bad idea, we should just vote. Who says we don't go into the woods near the school?"

Delilah was the only one who raised her hand, and I thought that would be the end, and we could go to our destination without any unrest.

"Okay, and who thinks we should go to the woods near the school?"

Everyone in the back seats raised their hand, and Gabriel raised his own hand up front, and he smirked at Delilah, who gave an annoyed look to all of us.

My hand started to shake a little more violently than it normally does, and I hoped no one would notice, but since it's my right hand, I can hide it from everyone else.

As we approached the school, my hand shook even more, so I left it between the seat and the door, hoping no one would notice that.

We all exited the truck, which was parked behind the school, and we trekked to the field, where multiple entrances to the woods were located.

Gabriel and Julia were walking together, which made me feel warm inside. Sibling love. It was always one of the best kinds in my opinion.

We continued down the field towards the looming trees. We decided to take the path that would usually lead you to Prince Hill, but we would be going deep into the woods.

After attempts to make it through the undergrowth, we decided just to be a little deeper, but could still find the baseball field.

There was a clearing near the baseball field anyway, so we just decided to set up an encampment there.

"Okay, so just put your stuff down, and we can find out how to set this up," Gabriel ordered, and we all obeyed, except for Delilah, who seemed annoyed she wasn't the leader she had seemed to be obsessed with being.

"Delilah, just put your stuff down, too." Gabriel sighed and gave her a dirty look because she was being difficult for no good reason.

Delilah ended up putting her stuff down, too, and we came up with a plan of action. "So, we're going to put tarps up along these trees, and set up two large tents under said tarps, to keep us protected from the rain, and we can also put weapons and other supplies in those tents as well."

We agreed on the plan and got to work. Dimitri, Julia, and I worked on the tarps, whilst the others were working on the tents.

The sun began to set when we finished, which I thought was pretty good, because now we can test out a small fire to cook the food Gabriel got.

Dimitri grabbed some cans of soup and handed them to Gabriel, who had started a small fire.

"Okay, but do we need to eat soup?" Delilah complained.

"Do you need to be a complaining little bitch right now?" Dimitri retaliated.

Delilah's face turned red, and she stormed off into the girls' tent.

"I have wanted to say that to her for so long, you guys have no idea." Dimitri smiled at us, and as the others smiled back, I winced.

I didn't know how to tell someone to back off and stop being rude or anything, but people like Dimitri make it look incredibly easy.

"How do you guys make retaliation look so easy?" I asked them.

The others shrugged, and I just sat on a nearby rock.

"It's okay, Livia." Dimitri walked over to where I was, comforting me.

"A lot of people can't retort well at first, but eventually, over time, it will get easier."

I smiled at him, and I was tempted to kiss him, but instead, he helped me up, and we went to retrieve a can of soup.

As I ate my soup, I wondered about how I could cope and completely process some of the most recent events.

Maybe I could draw in the dirt? Or maybe I could find something sharp and carve into trees? Like an "L + D" in a heart or something?

I kept those ideas in the back of my head, so I could at least try them one day.

I finished my soup, and we all handed Gabriel our empty cans, and Gabriel placed them in a black trash bag, even though we didn't have anywhere to put it.

Delilah hadn't eaten that night, but no one really gave a shit. We then went to sleep in our new little home during the hell known as World War III.

As I lay in a sleeping bag, I realized we hadn't done the "Tradition Time," and no one seemed to notice.

***

My mind was constantly thinking of the worst possible scenarios that could happen during the night.

I couldn't sleep, but I didn't want to leave the tent, because wild animals could easily kill me.

I knew most of the bad things in my head were most likely never going to happen, but I constantly worried I would lose someone, like Julia or Dimitri.

What time is it? I wondered as the night seemed to be infinite. Time was slowing, and all I could do was just stare at the roof of the tent.

I had taken a liking to Julia. The next morning, I was going to try to spend the day getting to know her.

I glanced over at Julia, whose breathing was peaceful and slow. Delilah, on the other hand, was breathing way faster and shallower.

The way the two were complete opposites was somewhat comforting for me. I don't know why, but it was kinda cool.

I wished I could spot the moon, but I could see some of the forest outside the tent, which was illuminated by the moonlight.

Eventually, I must have fallen asleep, because after a blink, it was morning.

I haven't really kept track of how many days it's been, but I know it's the middle of August.

"Breakfast!" I heard Gabriel call as Julia and Delilah got out of the sleeping bags, yawning. I managed to get myself out of the tent and over to some logs Dimitri hauled over. "Thanks, Dimitri!" I called over to him as he grabbed another to put across from the other. "Thanks, Gabriel, for breakfast." I smiled at Gabriel, who gave me a half smile.

I think Gabriel and I could be considered friends, maybe? I'm not sure, but I definitely want to become friends with Julia.

As we ate, I wondered what kind of berries Gabriel used to make the delicious smoothie-like substance in the bowls he must have carved the night before.

It honestly tasted like blueberries, strawberries, and blackberries, but there could be some more.

We continued eating, and I caught Julia glancing at me.

"Yes?" I asked her, still eating the berry thing. "I was just wondering if we could go foraging together, maybe fish?" Julia hid her smile, but was unsuccessful after a second.

"Oh sure!" I responded, smiling.

After we ate, I gathered some bait and baskets for fish and berries, as Julia grabbed a pair of fishing poles that Gabriel had.

As Julia and I gathered supplies for our little trip, I caught Delilah glaring at the two of us together, and I wondered what her problem was.

"So, you ready?" I asked Julia, who nodded in response.

We started walking towards a river we had all discovered while trying to find the perfect place to keep ourselves from dying. "So, I don't know why, but I kinda feel like Delilah's mad that we're hanging out," Julia mentioned as the sound of dead leaves crunched under our feet.

It wasn't even fall, but dead leaves plagued the ground, and the temperatures were quite high. It was the middle of August. "I know, right? She was glaring at us as we gathered our supplies." I responded, shuddering.

"But why?" Julia asked rhetorically, her brow furrowing.

"I wonder if it's because she's not the leader."

We both nodded, as that was the most likely answer out of the many possibilities.

We reached the river and set up the fishing poles with bait. As we waited for the fish to bite, Julia turned to me.

"Do you know how to sing?" she asked randomly.

"Um, yes, but I'm not that good." I smiled meekly, knowing she would judge me. "Can I hear you?" Julia's eyes widened, smiling at me, which gave me some confidence.

"What song?" I asked with a laugh. "Any song from or related to the Hunger Games," Julia responded almost immediately. "Ok then." I cleared my throat and sang "Safe and Sound" by Taylor Swift.

"That was amazing!" Julia exclaimed, almost dropping her fishing pole.

"No, it wasn't, but thank you for the compliments." I smiled back at her, and the sun illuminated our beams through the leaves. "You know, the life we're all living right now isn't so different from the world of The Hunger Games. I mean, we have to avoid a bunch of other people, like the tributes; we've formed an alliance with each other, just like the careers or Katniss' alliance with Peeta or Rue." "Oh my god, you're right," Julia said, her jaw dropping.

Eventually, we filled our baskets with fish and berries, and whilst walking back laughing, we spotted a deer just in time before it ran away.

We returned to the camp, where Dimitri, Gabriel, and Isaac were sitting, looking annoyed about something.

"What's going on?" Julia asked.

"Delilah ran away. Left this note." Dimitri handed us a note, sighing at it.

Dear Bastards…

I literally CANNOT deal with the toxicity you guys bring into the group, especially after we got Dumbass Raymond and Livia the Betrayer. I am traveling to Canada. At least there I won't be treated like the hated child. Have fun being toxic bitches!

-Delilah, who might as well be dead now

After I read it, I felt my blood boil. How could she call us "bastards", call me a "betrayer", and act like she's hated, when I didn't even do anything?

She called us toxic when she's been the only one with a problem. I'm honestly happy she's not causing any more big fusses, but I do know that she'll probably come back.

She's like a child who says they'll run away, and then return for dinner. I doubt she'd get to Canada, and if anything, she'll die out there.

"How do you guys feel about this?" I asked. "I think it's bullshit. She'll be back for supper." Gabriel responded, scoffing.

"I think she's a massive hypocritical bitch for calling us 'toxic bitches' and calling you a

'betrayer' when you didn't do anything." Dimitri said, laughing.

"I think she's messed up in the head, personally. She's been the one with a problem the whole time." Julia muttered.

"Personally, I think she'll either die if she actually does end up trying to get to Canada, or she'll come back for dinner, like what Gabriel said," Isaac responded, throwing his hands up like he was being arrested.

I didn't want to go look for her, but something in my head was telling me to. "I don't want to, but I feel as though we should look for her, just in case," I said, preparing for ridicule.

"We really shouldn't." Julia crossed her arms. "Yeah. Livia, we know you're all about doing the right thing and whatnot, but we really should just let her come back on her own. Actually, tell you what. If she isn't back tomorrow, we'll go check around here." Dimitri responded to me.

That night, I fell asleep, knowing we would have to find Delilah in the morning.

Everyone was noticeably frustrated the next morning, the reason being quite obvious. Delilah didn't return last night, and I have no idea whether or not I should consider it a good thing or a bad thing.

On one hand, Delilah's a manipulative little bitch, and we'd all love not to see her come back.

Then, on the other hand, it would actually be pretty important to make sure she's either alive or dead, so we should just make sure she is dead.

It was early, though. About seven a.m., and the sun was still rising, and the sky was the palest blue I've ever seen.

Julia had gotten up before me and was cooking the berries we had found the day before in the pot Gabriel had.

I think Julia was making some sort of jam or something, because she kept checking to make sure it was melted, and was asking.

Gabriel, if it was, and if she was blind. "Good morning, Julia." I yawned and stretched as I approached her.

"Not really a 'good' morning, but I get what you mean." Julia smiled at me, a half-smile.

I wondered if Julia felt as though she needed to conceal feelings, sending a feeling of familiarity to me.

I decided to talk to her about that, knowing she would probably trust Gabriel more, but then again, she did ask me to hang out with her yesterday.

Julia eventually put out the fire, letting the strange concoction of berries sit in the pot. "What were you making?" I asked her, and the feeling of awkwardness of the silence disappeared.

"A jam recipe from my da-adopted dad." Julia's eyes widened, but then returned to the normal deer eyes I knew.

So she's adopted. That makes more sense, since Gabriel and Julia don't really look related.

I knew something was going on. Maybe after breakfast, I'll take her aside and try to help her out.

Dimitri brought out everyone's wooden bowls and some spoons. Gabriel constantly checked the pot, smiling, and then went back to keeping animals and bugs away from the pot.

"Breakfast is ready!" Gabriel announced, and Isaac returned from the tent, and we all sat.

Gabriel passed out bowls of the newly cooled jam, which tasted quite good.

The blend of gooseberries, blueberries, cloudberries, blackberries, and huckleberries created a taste unlike anything I have ever tasted.

"This is really good, Julia!" I placed another spoonful in my mouth, feeling heaven in my mouth; the title had only been reserved for pasta.

"Thanks!" Julia said, with a small mouthful of jam in her mouth.

Another thing I'm sure everyone was excited about with Delilah gone was definitely manners. If Delilah were here, then everyone would be pestered about manners.

Hair too. Pretty much everyone's hair here was an absolute mess in Delilah's eyes, which was strange, because she wakes up with messy hair; she just obsesses over it early in the morning.

Delilah's opinion on hair and mannerisms is weird because it's World War III, so no one should really care about the dumb shit like hair being messy and whatnot all the time.

As we ate, Dimitri suddenly decided to mention the notions.

"I mean, if the bitch was here, then we'd be ridiculed for our 'messy' hair, our manners, and a bunch of other nonsense."

Everyone nodded in agreement, smiling at the absence of Delilah.

"You all wanna know the reason why no one wants to even talk to her?"

We nodded excessively, wanting to know Dimitri's theory on why. Dimitri always knows that shit.

"It's because whenever someone talks to her, whether it be about something random or if they needed someone to talk to about their feelings or something, she'll always say that her life was way worse."

"I can say for a fact that as a person who needed support, she actually said that to me," I mentioned.

"Did she also mention how her life was worse because of a 'whole class,' as in a group of girls making up a secret language just to talk shit about Delilah?" Dimitri asked me, smiling, knowing I had told him about that. "Yes. *And* she probably deserved it too!" I laughed, and Dimitri continued.

"Also, one day, we were in C period, and Kendra Palm accidentally bumped into Delilah and apologized, but Delilah was like, "Oh my god, stop being so rude to me!' Like, Kendra apologized and stuff!"

We all laughed at the stupidity of Delilah, and personally, I kinda wanted to find Delilah just so I could mention these things and laugh at how hypocritical she is.

Wait. I thought. That's not good. I shouldn't do it. But she deserves it.

I debated the notion, thinking of how it could be considered bad and how it could be justified.

Everyone finished their jam, and we all stretched from sitting on the logs, and it was probably eight a.m.

I took Julia aside, near the camp, but far enough that no one would hear us.

"Hey. You alright?" I asked, concerned for her. "Yeah, I'm fine!" Julia responded with a slight twitch in one of her eyes.

"I can tell you're not, so if you need anyone to support you, I'm here, Isaac's here, Dimitri's here, and even Gabriel." I smiled, hoping she would be alright.

"What's wrong?" I asked her. She started crying.

"I kinda feel guilty for Delilah leaving. And what if anyone dies?" Julia's deer eyes enlarged, and I felt sympathy for her. "It's okay. None of us is going to die. Delilah has a way to get into our heads and make us feel guilty, but we need to remember that she's done worse things than we ever have."

Julia looked up, hesitated, and then smiled at me.

"It'll take time, and hell, I'm still learning to keep those thoughts under control, but with time and support from real friends and family, for you, it could be Gabriel, or literally anyone here. Just remember, you'd never do anything that's even close to the kind of things Delilah's done."

We smiled at each other, knowing what we needed to do.

We returned to the camp, everyone gathering some supplies for the search, and Julia and I joined in as well.

I knew Julia's or my own thoughts would stop immediately, or even in a day, but I think I really helped Julia out, at least for now. After gathering the supplies, we set out to check if Delilah, a manipulative, toxic, and extremely defensive bitch, was dead or alive.

Chapter 7:

I assume it's almost eleven now, and we haven't been able to find her. We've been hiking in the woods for about an hour now, and we haven't found anything showing signs of Delilah being there.

I'm not sure why we haven't given up yet, but maybe it means we're still mentally at the service of Delilah and her toxicity.

"Guys, we haven't found any trace of her. We should probably go back." I finally spoke up, and the weight of the world seemed to leave my body, and seemed also to leave everyone else. "Oh my god, I am so happy someone said something." Gabriel sighed, smiling. "I didn't wanna say anything." Isaac's eyes widened as he spoke.

We all turned around to return to the camp, but as we headed back, I couldn't shake the feeling that something was wrong. "What's wrong? Are you alright?" Julia asked me, concern filling her face.

"I just feel like something's wrong." I looked around, making sure everyone was with us.

"I'm sure it's nothing," Julia reassured me.

I hope she's right, because the feeling was still there, just quieter. We continued our journey back to the encampment, and I still couldn't shake the feeling.

Something was wrong. Not sure what, but something. As we reached the camp, I needed to tell them.

Nothing seemed to be wrong with the camp, but I didn't care.

"Wait!"

Isaac and Julia, who had taken the front of the group, enthusiastically leading us back to the camp, had been scooped into an elaborate net trap covered with the dead leaves taking over the forest floor.

Delilah was nowhere to be found, which wasn't promising. I knew she had to have been the one behind this.

Gabriel took out a pocket knife and slowly cut through the rope, allowing Isaac and Julia to escape painlessly and easily. "I think we all know who's the one who set this up," Gabriel said with a knowing look on his face. "Delilah!" Gabriel boomed, the volume causing all of us to cover our ears.

I spotted Delilah hiding shamelessly behind a tree, and I rolled my eyes.

"Oh wow, she's so good at this little game of hide and seek, we can't find her!" I announced in a sarcastic tone, and when that didn't do the job, I knew exactly what to do.

"Imma mess up my hair and talk about how *amazing the others* are!"

I threw my hair around, trying to get it really messy, and just spat out a bunch of compliments about the others, which caused Delilah to storm out of her hiding place.

And, like a toddler, she threw a tantrum about my hair, saying it looked like a rat's nest, and even though it was World War III, I should still have some "dignity."

I tried my best not to laugh at how pathetic she was, but she knew my plan and was screaming at me for that.

"You hang out with those bastards way more than you do with me!"

As much as I knew this was incredibly stupid, I did feel quite guilty, but I continued to tell myself that she's a hypocritical, toxic, and narcissistic bitch, meaning I shouldn't feel guilty, but I still did.

She was still screaming at me, but I just felt annoyed and was kind of fed up with her shit, so I blurted out the first thing that came to mind.

"I don't care what you think is right, bitch." I sounded calm. Not angry, not upset, no voice cracks, and no choking. I had a straight face as well. I walked away from her, back to the camp, where I went into the tent, and contemplated what had just happened, while silently crying.

I could hear Dimitri screaming at Delilah for being a bitch, and I'm not sure how, but they seemed to sense that I was crying, meaning they were even angrier at her. It felt good. Knowing they were there for me. Julia came into the tent and hugged me. I returned the gesture as well and felt her tears dropping onto my shoulders.

"It's gonna be alright." She whispered, sniffling afterwards.

"I'm not sure if that's true or not," I whispered back, sniffling as well.

As the sounds of Dimitri, Gabriel, and Issac overpower Delilah with their volume, Julia and I emerged from the tent, faces stained with the tears we cried.

Dimitri and Gabriel were tying Delilah to a tree; the rope was pretty much impossible to break through, and they were unable to allow Delilah to slip through somehow.

Isaac was admiring her knife in his hands, inspecting the blood stains. Delilah had decided to keep on the edge of the blade, for dramatic effect, I assumed.

"So she's not going anywhere?" I asked Gabriel and Dimitri when they finished the tight knot. "Yep! No way she could ever break out of those ropes, and, even better, we made sure she wasn't able to speak either!" Dimitri gestured to a gagged Delilah, who you could tell was frowning, and we all waved at her with a smile on our faces, and she let out a muffled scream, trying to break free of the ropes around her. I felt better. Knowing they care, and also sharing the same opinion on someone, was something I loved.

It was lunch time, and we had some leftover fish from yesterday, when Julia and I went fishing. Thankfully, Gabriel had gotten loads of salt at Walmart, and we were able to keep food fresh.

Another reason why Ms. Zeega's class is useful. We learned about why salt was valuable in Africa and Europe.

As the fish cooked, Delilah's eyes glistened in the light of the fire, even though it was still daytime.

She glared at me, and I just tried not to look at her, but just the feeling of her staring into my soul was piercing.

It was as though her gaze was her knife, and I was stabbed. The knife went through my body and stabbed into the ground as well, making me unable to move.

I shuddered at the image. The fish finished cooking, and I announced lunch. As we ate, I could hear Delilah's muffled screams, probably about how we were eating the fish "wrong," but I didn't give a shit anymore.

When Dimitri finished, he took one part of the fish he didn't eat and force-fed it to Delilah, who resisted until she drooped over, defeated.

We all finished our fish, put the fire out, and retreated to our tents for the night, not caring whether or not Delilah would be eaten or mauled by any sort of creature.

Personally, I wished that she wouldn't die, but continuously be on the brink of death, wishing for its sweet release, but never grasping it.

That night, I was still in the woods, but it was daytime again; however, shadows plagued the forest as I was running.

Beside me, two taller and more muscular figures, whom I assumed were Gabriel and Dimitri, ran with me. There was someone else, someone I couldn't make out, but didn't fit the physicality of anyone else.

I couldn't stop running, and even worse, Julia and Isaac were nowhere to be seen. I wondered what was happening that was making us run like this.

Behind us, gunshots and shadows were following us. I heard a scream, and then the shadows and gunshots suddenly stopped.

I woke up, not used to Delilah not being in the tent with Julia and me. Julia was still asleep, so I let her sleep in. She looked like she could use it anyway.

I exit the tent, trying to be quiet and not wake anyone, especially Julia. I couldn't see anyone else outside, except for Delilah, who was still tied to the tree, thankfully.

Her eyes were like spears made of dark ice, stabbing me into one of the trees behind me. I shivered, but gave her a dirty look back. She was covered in bug bites, more than the ones the rest of us have gotten. It made sense, though. I mean, she was outside all night, more exposure to all the bugs, while we were in tents.

I took a basket and made my way into the woods. Searching for berries, hoping no one would wake up as I was out here.

For some reason, I wondered what I would be doing right now if none of this were happening.

Probably painting or drawing. I thought, my eyes scanning the perimeter. No berries so far, but I wasn't going to give up just yet.

Soon enough, I found a bush of blackberries, which intrigued me immediately. I picked some, getting enough for all of us, while also saving some for the wildlife.

I debated whether or not to go back to the camp or search for some more berries. I went searching for more berries and was scanning the forest for more berry bushes.

After searching for maybe five minutes, I finally found a cluster of different berry bushes. I made sure to identify which were poisonous and which were safe to eat.

I picked some of the wild strawberries and cloudberries, but sadly, the other berry bushes were poisonous, to my knowledge.

As I headed back to the camp, I hoped. Delilah was still tied up. I'm not sure why, but I just feel like somehow, in some way, she'll get out of the ropes.

With the camp in sight, I couldn't see any sign of Delilah being released, or escaped, or anyone being awake.

I set up the campfire, about to start making the berry concoction from earlier this week.

As the water was heating up, I crushed the berries with a pestle. The berries created a strange, dark orange color.

When the water started boiling, I poured the crushed berries in and stirred.

The water turned the same color as the crushed berries.

After about twenty minutes of stirring, the concoction was thick, and I stopped the fire, let the jam settle, but made sure no bugs would be able to get to it.

I went over to check on Delilah's ropes, which were thankfully still tight. Sadly, she seemed to have found a way to get the gag off. "*Psst.* Hey. Livia." Delilah whispered to me, but I ignored her.

"Oh! So you're just *too good* to even *look* at me,

now? *Wow!* Some friend *you* are!" I took a deep breath and continued to ignore her. Not even looking at her, either, like she said.

I have had validation that I *am*, in fact, a "good friend," so her words don't have as big an effect on me as they used to.

I still feel a little guilty, but thankfully, I'm able to suppress it far enough that it can't completely get to me.

Dimitri exited his tent due to Delilah screaming at me to get my attention, which wasn't exactly working in the way she intended. "Sorry about the noise, Dimitri," I said, trying to repress a smile, which wasn't working, especially since he caught on and was trying not to burst out laughing.

"You don't gotta be sorry, Livia." He said, slightly snickering at Delilah being an absolute menace right now.

Gabriel and Isaac came out soon after, yawning and obviously woken by Delilah's screaming.

"Wait, how'd she get the gag off?" Dimitri asked, genuinely concerned.

"I actually don't know. She had it on when I woke up, but when I returned with the berries, she had it off!" I said, still not even looking at her or even in her direction.

Dimitri shrugged it off and re-tied the scarf around Delilah's face to prevent her from talking.

Personally, the scarf looked like a bandana when Delilah slipped through it.

Now, Dimitri made it tighter and made sure Delilah didn't bite him, which she was trying to do.

I went to check on the jam, and it looked like it had set and had cooled off in the shade.

With the jam split between all of us, Julia had finally come out of the tent and didn't look as tired as she had before.

I think Delilah not being much of a problem anymore has helped her out a lot. I felt happy for Julia and handed her the bowl of jam, and she beamed at me.

As we all ate breakfast, I could just tell that Delilah was blinded in rage. And I was still not even looking in her direction.

"Hey, so what's the plan for today?" Julia asked, swallowing a spoonful of jam. "We need some more food, so I was thinking maybe Livia, Dimitri, and I could go fishing and or hunting," Isaac mentioned, and Dimitri and I nodded in agreement.

I still wasn't that close with Isaac for some reason, so it might be pretty good for me to get to know him better. Plus, Dimitri was going to be there too, which made everything even better.

We were still eating the jam, and I wondered what Gabriel and Julia would do while the rest of us were gone.

"What're you and Gabriel gonna do while the rest of us are gone?" I asked Julia, who shrugged.

"Maybe we could try to fortify this place a little more?" Gabriel suggested, shrugging as he ate. Julia nodded, her smile shining, despite all of the terrible events that have happened so far these past 4 months.

We all finished our jam and cleaned the bowls and spoons to make sure we could use them again.

Afterwards, I poured the jam into one of the containers Gabriel had gotten from Walmart months ago, and stored it in the area where we store the food, which was in the boys' tent.

Julia and I got dressed for the day in the tent, making sure to put our hair up, as we wouldn't want our hair getting in the way of what we were doing today.

Surprisingly, despite popular belief, not all girls take forever to get ready. We got ready in less than ten minutes, perhaps even less than five, and we were ready before the boys, which was even funnier.

After we all got dressed, Dimitri, Isaac, and I got the supplies required for our little adventure, and set off, waving at Gabriel and Julia, and began our hunt as they fortified.

Chapter 8:

It was honestly quite fun to trek through the woods with Isaac and Dimitri. The river was rushing a lot, so it was easier to locate it, since we could hear it from about a quarter-mile away.

I made sure to make it a clear memory of how to get back in case Dimitri or Isaac forgot.

We took out the fishing rods, attached the bait, and cast out into the rushing water. I wondered if this river could be connected to the brook in my old backyard.

Probably not, but it was an interesting thought, which *could* be possible, but there were many rivers in Connecticut, specifically in this area, the "Quiet Corner" of Connecticut, which meant that there were other rivers the brook could be connected to. A bite on my bait, and I reeled the fish up, and it was a sculpin. The frog-like head was a dead giveaway.

Isaac had then caught a herring, which looked pretty good. Dimitri had already caught 2 herrings and was about to reel in another fish.

I'm pretty sure Dimitri had the skills of a master fisherman, which kind of fit his demeanor.

"Wow," Isaac commented on Dimitri, who had just caught a sculpin.

I think an hour must have passed, because our asses were in pain after sitting on a small cliff edge by the river.

We packed up the fishing gear and placed the fish evenly in a basket that Dimitri brought and carried on his back.

I took out the Mauser M18 that had piqued my interest for the hunting part of this little field trip.

I made sure to make no sound, just as Isaac and Dimitri were, and held my rifle for whatever was out there.

I spotted a lone deer, eating some food in a clearing, and I gestured to Dimitri and Isaac.

They gave me a thumbs up, and I went closer, aiming the rifle right in the deer's chest. Once I was ready, I pulled the trigger. The deer fell over, shocked and dying, and I went in for the prize.

Dimitri and Isaac followed me, ready to harvest our meat.

"That was amazing, Livia!" Dimitri exclaimed, taking out a knife to skin the deer.

"Yeah!" Isaac beamed at me, taking out a basket-container like Dimitri's.

I felt proud of myself. I hadn't actually been able to kill something successfully; hell, I haven't actually used a gun before.

I smiled as I helped Isaac and Dimitri load the meat parts into the basket-container, all of us happy and satisfied.

"Should we go back or continue hunting?" I asked as we finished loading the last of the venison.

"I think this should be enough to last us a few days," Dimitri said confidently.

Isaac, Dimitri, and I proudly returned to the camp, with enough food to last us up to a week if we were lucky.

As we walked triumphantly back to the camp, I started feeling as though something, or someone, was watching us.

It was eerie, especially since the trees were thick in this area, so you couldn't easily see someone.

Thankfully, I was between Isaac and Dimitri, so if someone were following us, they wouldn't be directly behind me, but then that means they would be behind Dimitri, which was probably worse.

I tried to shake off the feeling, rationalizing with myself, like, who would be following us? No one would even come out here.

Which would make it the perfect place to stay, especially since soldiers are invading homes and stuff. I shivered.

"You alright, Livia?" Dimitri's voice made me jump, which made everything possibly worse. "Oh, yeah! I'm alright, just cold." I smiled, which wasn't convincing. He raised an eyebrow.

"Ok. What's *actually* going on with you?" Dimitri was good.

"*Fine.* I just feel as though someone is watching us, or following us."

"No one would be out here, though," Dimitri responded, his brow still raised.

"Which makes the forest the *perfect* place to hide from the soldiers and other people." "Ok. We're almost at the camp, and Julia and Gabriel have been working on fortifications, so we'll be alright." Dimitri smiled, trying to make me feel better, which was sweet.

"Ok. Thanks, by the way." "For what?" Dimitri asked.

"Making me feel a little better." I smiled at him, and he smiled in response as well.

We reached the camp, or at least what we thought was the camp, as there was a huge wooden wall with pointed tops.

We walked around the wall, eventually finding an entry.

"Hey, guys!" Isaac announced to Julia and Gabriel, who were working on this end.

"We honestly thought you'd be out longer. But you guys being here now means we have extra hands." Gabriel told us as he planted a pointed log against the wall.

Isaac and Dimitri unloaded the food as I put away all the supplies we took. I finished before them, which I found strange, but I could see them anyway, so I assumed it was probably fine.

I started helping Julia out, who seemed to have a bit of a hard time sharpening a log.

"Thanks, Livia." Julia smiled as she panted.

"Are your hands okay?" I asked, and her hands were shaking, and the fingertips were slightly bruised.

"I'm fine." She smiled again, her eyes slightly drooping, which kept me unconvinced.

"I think you should take a break. I'll take over the sharpening for now, and you can get some water and make sure your fingertips don't become a problem for you."

Julia sighed and nodded, her head down as she ventured to the tent, sending a thumbs up on the way.

As I sharpened the logs, Dimitri and Isaac walked over to Gabriel, who pointed to some axes to get more logs.

The two nodded profusely and got to work immediately.

I then realized that I have successfully not let Delilah cross my mind for most of the day, until now, but still!

We continued to work on the wall until lunch, where we all took a break, but then got right back to work.

We needed the protection from wild animals and whatever other potential threats were out there.

Once dinnertime came around, we had finally finished the wall.

We were all pretty shocked at how fast the day and the work went by.

Triumphant, we cheered as we ate dinner and fell asleep knowing we were safe and sound.

***

I can't sleep. I'm not sure what it is, but I woke up, and I can't fall asleep again. I mean, I know the *possible* causes, but I'm not sure which one it really is.

Stress. For one, it's the *third world war,* so it made sense, and two, we weren't *totally* sure of our protection, as people *could* find a way in, which probably made things worse. Anxiety, which is *really* similar to stress, but I think they're two different terms.

The fact that it's World War III makes everything terrible, and I'm thinking it could be a combination of all three, which would make sense, but whatever.

Even so, I should at least try to get myself tired, so I carefully and quietly left the tent, successfully not waking anybody up.

I could spot Delilah, who was somehow asleep, and honestly, I didn't care if I woke *her,* but I made sure to be quiet anyway.

Am I hungry? I asked myself, my stomach starting to hurt incredibly badly.

No. I need to do something else. I walked over to the designated area for bathroom business and made sure no one could see me.

I could hear the crickets outside, which emitted a sense of peace, even though we were all living in a world where we could be nuked at any moment.

Soldiers could find us easily, too, which could be worse, depending on what they would do to us.

Which reminded me of Sophia Saonn.

What had the soldiers done to her? I mean, she was pretty annoying, but if something *really bad* happened, then I don't want the soldiers to find us.

I'm not actually sure what the girls meant when they talked about what had happened to Sophia Saonn, because they were quite vague.

Well, honestly, I didn't blame the girls for being vague. It was probably horrifying to see it happening, even if it was someone you didn't like.

Personally, whatever horrible thing happened, I would *never* wish it on my worst enemy. Maybe not even Delilah.

But what about Avery Marengo? She seemed like she could survive, but where was she? I kinda wanted her to be here with us, and I'm not really sure why.

I finished up and made sure no one could see me still, and thankfully, no one could. As I made my way back to the tent, out of the corner of my eye, I could see Delilah going back to sleep, but in a dramatic way, so I think she was faking it.

I rolled my eyes and went back inside the tent, where Julia hadn't woken up yet, which was amazing.

As I got back into the sleeping bag, I wondered what kind of life Julia had before all of this.

I felt myself falling asleep, which was what I wanted, so I felt satisfied.

My eyes closed, and I felt waves of unconsciousness washing me away, and as the last wisps of consciousness flew away from me, my mind flooded with anxiety-filled thoughts, which brought me back to consciousness.

I hated it when this happened. I'll be on the brink of sleep, and my mind will go to some kind of scenario where someone will get hurt, or something bad will happen, and I'll be kept awake.

Damn. Now I have to deal with this again. I lay in the sleeping bag, my eyes twitching slightly at every negative thought caused by anxiety that came into my mind. *Seriously. Why the actual hell do people have to deal with this?* I thought angrily, *It's so annoying!*

As I lay in the sleeping bag, irritated by the thoughts keeping me awake, I wondered if any of my friends had to deal with this also.

If anything, it would be either Gabriel or Isaac. I thought about analyzing the memories I have of them.

Hmm. Maybe I could imagine some ASMR, and then I could trick my brain into falling asleep while it's distracted!

It seemed like a good idea until I realized it was quite difficult.

Ugh. Why right now? When are we all doing amazing in this goddamn war? I went back to being irritated, just lying in the sleeping bag, with insomnia and the hatred for said insomnia.

Maybe I should just try to relax and not be so tense! I thought, smiling to myself.

I breathed slowly and deeply, relaxing my muscles, and imagining I was floating on a cloud or in the water.

The water moved me slowly and calmly. The water wasn't a river. It was some infinite space of water, and I'm not sure what that could classify as.

Maybe an ocean? Maybe a really big pool? The water was clear, and nothing seemed ominous or anything, so I relaxed a little more. The water felt gentle, and little waves seemed to wash against my legs, as if I were on a beach now, but all I could see was a beautiful blue sky, no sun, but all the light I needed for it not to be too bright, but bright enough so I could see.

As the water brushed against my legs, and I drifted in the infinite space, I felt myself finally letting go of consciousness, and my mind plunging into a deep sleep.

Suddenly, the scene changed. I was back to running, Gabriel and Dimitri beside me, and the mysterious young woman as well, and Delilah, Isaac, and Julia were nowhere to be seen.

I should ask Gabriel and Dimitri what happened to make us run, and also why Isaac and Julia weren't here. I don't really care what happened to Delilah.

"What happened to Isaac and Julia?" I asked them, who didn't turn back to face me, as though they didn't hear me, or I hadn't even spoken at all, but a loud ringing noise suddenly flooded my ears, and it hurt really badly.

Suddenly, shadows surrounded me, and then I was transported back to the water. I felt confused, scared, and overwhelmed by what had just occurred.

I immediately woke up, panting and sweating my ass off. I adjusted to the world around me, being in the tent, and lay back down. "I don't know what the hell that was, but I know that I'm a total loser for talking to myself again." I looked down upon myself for that, as it was totally weird, and if anybody found out, they'd probably abandon me or something.

I continued to regulate my breathing, and eventually, I fell back asleep, thankfully.

Chapter 9:

Morning has arrived, and I feel sleep-deprived. Julia had already gotten up, but I felt terrible. I had to get up, though. I groaned as I groggily sat up and got out of my sleeping bag, my hair obviously an absolute mess, but I didn't care.

Gabriel was making breakfast. I couldn't see what it was, but it smelled good. Julia and Isaac were talking to Gabriel, but Dimitri wasn't in my line of sight.

Delilah was there, but Dimitri wasn't here. *Maybe he's just hunting....* I thought, *but we already got a lot of food yesterday.* I looked around, trying to spot him, but I still couldn't find him.

Maybe he's in the boys' tent. That's probably it. I rubbed my eyes and yawned as I made my way over to Isaac and Julia. "What're you guys talking about?" I asked, trying to smile through the pain of being awake.

"What we wanted to be when we grew up, before all of this." Julia gestured with her hand, her teeth gritting.

"I wanted to be…" Isaac said, blushing slightly. "You don't gotta be embarrassed by that," I said, smiling at him to cheer him up, but I think he could tell that I wasn't fine, because he suddenly looked concerned.

"You alright, Livia?" He asked, his eyes widening with fear.

"Just feel a little tired. Couldn't really sleep last night." I smiled at him, hoping to convince him that I was okay.

"Okay then." He said slowly, giving me a suspicious look.

"I wanted to be a singer!" Julia blurted out, trying to break any tension.

"So is that connected to when you asked me to sing for you?" I asked.

"Yeah…" Julia blushed, looking at the forest floor.

"That makes a lot of sense!" I responded, feeling a slight weight of the unknown floating off of me.

"What did you wanna be, Livia?" Isaac asked, turning towards me.

"Honestly, I wanted to be an author." I smiled, reminiscing about the past, the time when I didn't even know this was gonna happen. It was an amazing part of my life, before I discovered the world and learned how it worked.

I envied my past, but lots of embarrassing things happened, and I couldn't *possibly* do anything embarrassing *now,* because no one who judged me before was around me anymore.

Maybe…. this wasn't so-No! I can't think that. People have probably died from this! I chastised myself, knowing I shouldn't think that this could even *remotely* be a good thing, but honestly, it's better than being given dirty looks and looked down upon for past events and actions that shouldn't define me, but the kids I know really don't think anyone can change, which is completely stupid.

I mean, they *are* dumbasses when it comes to many things, but it just pains me that they could be so ignorant, dense, and overall simple-minded.

I mean, lots of people in this world are, but still!

"That's so cool!" Julia and Isaac's eyes widened and beamed at me.

"I know what *I* wanted to be when I grew up!" Dimitri appeared behind me, and I jumped in surprise.

"Livia's husband!" He smirked at me, and I just tried to hide my face, which was obviously red from blushing too much.

"Oh my god, stop! What did you *actually* want to be?" I laughed as I spoke. I could barely breathe, so I tried to calm myself.

"Marines." Dimitri responded, his face morphing into a "stoic" face, making us burst out laughing.

"If you guys are done being weird, it's breakfast time." Gabriel raised his eyebrow at our antics and passed plates of eggs and some of the venison from the deer I shot.

"Wait," Isaac put his plate next to him, "where'd you get eggs?"

"I went out early to find something for breakfast, since it's a bit of a special occasion today, if anybody catches my drift, and I found some chickens for some reason, and I took the eggs." Gabriel stared at Julia in a knowing way, and she smiled.

"Happy birthday, Gabriel!" she announced excitedly.

"Wait, wait, wait. Is it your *birthday?*" Dimitri gave him a look of disbelief.

"Yep," Gabriel responded. "August 24, 2010." "Wow. So that makes you fifteen?" I asked. "That's right." Gabriel said proudly, "I'm so old."

"Wait. When were any of *you* guys born?" I asked. I hadn't actually known when the rest of them were born.

"June 18, 2011," Dimitri responded, as though he were speedrunning this.

I was a little concerned, but I decided to ignore it.

"April 10, 2013," Julia responded, smiling without a trace of hesitance.

"June 15, 2011," Isaac responded, slight hesitancy hidden within his tone.

"I know Delilah was born April 4, 2011," I said, feeling good, knowing the most basic information anyone could know about their friends.

"What about you, Livia?" Julia asked everyone, turning towards me, and I gulped, feeling slightly nervous about it.

"June 22, 2011," I responded, feeling warm inside. We were all bonding closer and closer, and that felt better than anything else in my life.

"Cool!" Julia responded.

"So, what're we gonna do today?" Isaac asked as we finished our eggs quickly so that they wouldn't be *too* cold.

"It's been some months, we should send a group to try to scout the town, make sure if it's safe or not, and go from there," Gabriel informed us, after finishing his plate.

"Okay then. Who's gonna go?" Dimitri asked, almost done with his plate.

"I'm thinking it should be a small group of people who know how to be stealthy, and can easily get around quickly, while also being able to defend themselves if they come into contact with someone hostile." Gabriel thought for a moment.

"I'm thinking, Dimitri, definitely. You'd be perfect for the defense part, and I'm sure you could be stealthy, on account of the fact that you were interested in the Marines when you were younger." Gabriel looked at the rest of us, thinking hard.

"Livia, you'd be pretty stealthy, and…. maybe Julia?" Gabriel shrugged, trying to get some kind of feedback.

"I mean, Julia would be perfect, but is it her first time?" Dimitri inquired.

"No, actually." Isaac chimed in, smiling at Julia, who seemed proud of herself.

"Well, we should do this then," Dimitri stated, standing up, and I did the same, along with Julia.

"Let's do this," I said excitedly as we loaded some guns, making sure to have tons of ammo, in case something were to happen.

As we departed towards town, I started to worry. There was a high chance we could die. The school was disappearing behind the trees as we walked the desolate road towards the town.

"So, which part of town should we go to? I mean, like, should we go to the Town Hall area? Or the Walmart area?" I asked Dimitri, who was leading us.

"I'm thinking we should go to the Walmart area first, and if we find something, we'll go back. If not, then we go to the Town Hall area, if we have time." Dimitri responded, his eyes shifting around the area quickly.

We continued towards Prince Hill Road, which would lead us to an intersection close to Delilah's house and a direct road to Walmart. It'd take us almost an hour to get there on foot, so we packed water and food with us in case we got stuck out here.

I think it's ten a.m. now, so by the time we get there, it'll probably be eleven, giving us about an hour or two to search and have enough time to search the Town Hall area.

As we made our way up the asphalt road, the paint fading, I wondered if we were going to find something.

"Do you think we'll find anything interesting?" I asked Julia.

"I'm not sure." She responded, shrugging her shoulders.

"Maybe we'll find some other survivors?" I suggested, feeling a little scared. Like, what if they were dangerous?

"Doubt it." Dimitri said, "I mean, if we *did,* let's just hope they aren't hostile."

I felt a little better, but I could still be right about finding other people like us, but they were most likely not gonna be so friendly to us.

Even if they were people we *knew,* which was unlikely, but it's a small town, so that it *could* happen, they would *still* be likely not to be nice.

Once, I imagined what would happen if our entire grade were stranded on a random island out in the middle of the Pacific or something, and we had to build a successful society there, at least until someone found us. I knew that they were crazy, so I knew they would definitely try to band together and kill the people they hated, so I would just hide somewhere to make sure no one tried to kill me.

I also knew that people would *definitely* sacrifice Sophia Saonn, because I would hear them talking shit about her every day.

People even created something similar to the "Cheese Touch," which is similar to a game of tag, but you can be safe from it by crossing two fingers; however, it was spread by anyone in contact with Sophia Saonn.

I remember a couple of years ago, Isaac and I both hated Jacob Urbanite, so we created the "Jacob Touch," which was basically the "Cheese Touch," but you got it if you came into contact with Jacob, or someone who was in contact with Jacob, touched you.

No one knew it was Isaac and me who actually started it, because it took the grade by storm, and eventually, the teachers caught wind of it, and got everyone together, and informed us that they figured it out, but Isaac and I never got in trouble, so we assume that no one knows.

It stopped, but Isaac and I were satisfied with the controversies and how fast it spread. I wondered if anyone would sacrifice Jacob, but his "friends" might keep him alive, but then I remembered something a kid named Aaron Brecken told me once: "No one here has friends, just people they tolerate enough to hang out with."

Then that means it could be everyone for themselves, except maybe my friends, but I'm always second-guessing myself whenever loyalty comes up for friends.

The concept of loyalty is strange, because I try to convince myself that my friends are real, but a voice in the back of my mind has its doubts.

Suddenly, I'm wondering about trying to give Delilah a chance to change and not be so toxic if I just talk to her, but no one would agree.

I know no one would want to give her another chance, but maybe it would be healthy for *everyone,* even Delilah, to give her another chance, and make sure she means it if she agrees to change her toxic demeanor.

Actually, I'm wondering why no one has killed her yet.

They all hate her, but why didn't they kill her instead of tying her to the tree and tying a scarf-thing around her mouth to make sure she can't talk?

We've reached the two options for Prince Hill Road, and to get to Walmart faster, we go straight, which leads to the intersection with Delilah's house.

I think we still have about maybe thirty or so minutes left before we reach the Walmart area.

"Hey, is something wrong?" I asked Julia, who looked a little concerned about something. "Yeah, just worried if we find someone mean." Julia smiled at me, and I figured she could be lying, but I shouldn't push her to talk about something she didn't wanna talk about.

We continued walking, and the clouds continued to cover the sky ominously.

I shivered, a slight breeze crawling up my spine as my eyes darted around my surroundings, making sure no one was going to snipe us or something.

I couldn't see anyone, hidden or otherwise, which made me even more fearful. The unknown factor in most phenomena always scared me greatly.

After what seemed like forever, we had finally reached the intersection near Delilah's house.

We turned right, towards Walmart, and headed down the long and seemingly endless road.

The road really *did* seem long and endless on foot, especially since we had always been in *some* kind of vehicle, whether it be a bus, car, or anything else; it hadn't always been so long.

I knew it would be a long trip, but with the whole town being so *quiet*, I didn't expect it to seem *that* long.

I could see Walmart and everything else in the distance, but several vehicles were stationed down the hill.

Thankfully, we ducked behind some bushes before someone spotted us, because there were a lot of soldiers down there, too. "What is happening?" I asked Dimitri, hoping he had some kind of idea, but he seemed as speechless as Julia and I were.

"Yeah, let's just go see if the Town Hall area's just as crowded..." Dimitri trailed off as he ran the other way, gesturing to us to follow him.

I had no idea what was going on down there. Hell, *Dimitri* doesn't seem to know either! I just know that if *Dimitri* doesn't want to investigate further, it must be something *very bad.*

Chapter 10:

As we ran up the road, we started to slow down. It was tiring for us to continue running.

We started panting too, and sweat started to drip down our faces, probably due to the hot August heat, the confusion and stress from the huge amounts of soldiers in the Walmart area, and also us just bolting along the road *uphill.*

Thankfully, no soldiers had seen us, so we assumed we would be safe for now, but we *needed* to know if any soldiers were gathering in the Town Hall area.

We didn't know what they were doing, but whatever it was, it couldn't be good, since they *were* trying to kill us during our last encounter.

The Town Hall area was about thirty minutes away from us right now, so we needed to hurry.

As we sped walked to the Town Hall, I couldn't help but notice some things I hadn't noticed before about my surroundings.

There were more trees than I thought, and there was a *ton* of grass past the trees on the side of the road.

As we continued, the buildup of confusion and stress made me go faster, and I eventually caught up with Dimitri, and Julia followed behind me, thankfully close.

The road felt even longer than when we were walking on it. I think that says a lot, since we're going faster than we did earlier.

It felt strange, and I was starting to run out of breath, but I carried on. I *had* to carry on with the others. If we stopped, we might be unprepared for something bad.

I wondered what would happen if my legs just randomly stopped, which felt plausible, as my legs were starting to get sore from running constantly for about ten minutes now.

I could see a little bit of the Town Hall down the hill, and Dimitri held out his arms, signaling us to stop.

Julia and I were panting, Dimitri was slightly breathing irregularly, and he seemed to be thinking of something.

"What do we do?" I asked Dimitri, hoping he had a plan.

"We advance in the vegetation." He responded, jogging to some trees and bushes close by.

Julia and I followed his lead, making sure we weren't seen by any soldiers or anybody, really, and just making sure we were sticking together.

We spotted some soldiers outside the Town Hall, talking about something.

Suddenly, the soldiers went inside the Town Hall, looking serious, unlike when they were talking.

We decided to sneak into the Town Hall, but first, we had to make sure no one else was outside, and then, we left our bags in the bushes, concealed from sight, and made our way into the Town Hall.

A supposed "leader," I guess, stood behind a podium in the center of the room and began some sort of speech.

After about five minutes, the crowd of soldiers cheered, and Dimitri gave Julia and me widened eyes.

"What?" I whispered.

"They're gonna burn down the forest, because since they think people won't go there, it's the perfect place to find people," Dimitri whispered back.

We snuck away from the crowd, making sure no one could spot us in the blinding light.

Thankfully, we got away before anyone noticed, and we ran back to the camp immediately.

Even more thankfully, it only took about fifteen minutes to get to Prince Hill Park, in which the forest was directly connected to the one near the baseball field at the middle school. The woods were infested with bugs, and it was really annoying to keep them out of our eyes, noses, and mouths.

For some reason, bugs kept trying to get into my ears, which I found incredibly weird, but not as weird as it was annoying.

We continued our way towards the school, down a dirt pathway, making sure no one was following us.

Soon, we reached the school, and we made our way towards the baseball field.

The sun was high in the center of the sky, and we needed to tell Gabriel and Isaac soon, or we could be in huge danger.

Plus, Dimitri didn't seem to know when they were gonna do it *exactly*, but judging by how scared he looked, it's most likely soon. "Gabriel! Isaac!" Dimitri shouted as we entered the encampment.

"What's wrong?" Gabriel asked, sounding a little concerned.

"The soldiers," I said, as we were still panting from running so long.

"What about the soldiers?" Isaac asked, his voice and eyes showing all signs of fear.

"They're gonna burn down the forest..." Julia said, monotone and looking as though she had seen a ghost.

"Julia, are you alright?" Gabriel bent down to her level, placing his hand gently on her shoulder.

"Y-yeah…I think so." She responded, her face still distraught.

"Hey, is it okay if I talk to Delilah about something?" I asked, hoping they wouldn't disagree.

"Why?" Julia asked, going from distressed to confused in the blink of an eye.

"I kind of think it might be a good idea to give Delilah maybe a second chance, or try to make sure she's faithful if she says she'll change." I held my breath.

"You know what? We could use the extra hand or mind for whatever we're gonna do to prepare for this." Gabriel responded, shrugging as we all walked over to the tree where Delilah was staring at us, confused, as Dimitri unbound the scarf around her face.

"Delilah," I started, "We've been talking, and we think it would be healthy for *all* of us if you promise to change, and we'll untie you, and we can all survive and work together to keep

ourselves safe from the soldiers."

Delilah stared at all of our faces, her eyes wide, and just laughed.

"You guys *don't* trust me enough to do this." Delilah pointed out.

"I mean-"

"No, no, no. I mean it. You guys aren't going to trust me, so I refuse your offer." Delilah looked away, and I felt hopeless, but then an idea came into my mind.

"Well, I guess *we'll* be the ones to survive the fire that will burn the whole forest to the ground." I shrugged, and everyone else played along.

"Wait! I didn't know that part!" Delilah pleaded.

"No, you've seemed to have made your decision, and I respect it."

"No, no, no, wait! I changed my mind! I promise I'll change! I promise I'll be a better person! I promise I'll help out in any way I can!" Delilah's eyes began to tear up, and I smiled and nodded.

"Okay then. Now all we need to do is figure out a strategy."

"The soldiers didn't give us a time frame, sadly, so they could be here any day now," Gabriel announced, pacing in front of us as we focused intensely.

"We need to hold down the fort," Isaac said, "we spent *too* much time in this base to make sure we could survive. We can't just abandon it."

"Well, Isaac, we might have emotional attachments to this place, but it's made of wood. No matter what we do, we're gonna have to leave it eventually." Delilah chimed in response.

"You guys don't understand. Before all of this, you know what I had for an 'emotional attachment?' Nothing! Absolutely nothing! The only thing that could even *slightly count* would be a dog that was alive for a week before it died of a goddamn disease!" Isaac lashed out towards us.

My eyes burned as I fought back tears. That was genuinely a *good* reason to want to stay, but we just *couldn't.*

"But Isaac-"

"No, Julia!" Isaac cut her off, "I actually mean it. I will *not* let *another* place of memories get destroyed like everything, and everyone else did!" Isaac stormed out of the camp, the rest of us sitting there, speechless.

Time was running out, and we still needed to find out where we were gonna go, or what would happen when it came to Isaac. The sun began to set, and we were too tired to continue seeking refuge or some way to preserve ourselves at least.

Isaac hadn't come out, but when we checked the boys' tent at dinnertime, he wasn't there. We assumed he needed to walk in the woods, and we just hoped he would be alright. It felt weird to have Delilah in the tent with us again, and it felt a little *exciting*, too. I don't think Julia took Isaac's lashing out at her so well. We tried telling her it was most likely *not* personal, but she still seemed depressed.

I felt bad for Julia. Isaac was like a best friend to her. They were so *close*, and she mustn't have expected it ever to happen, but it did, and that *really* must have broken her.

The clutches of unconsciousness were grabbing at me, and darkness fell upon the world, and crickets continued to click and sing as I fell asleep.

The place I woke up in was strange, to say the least.

It was some sort of forest. Pine trees everywhere, unlike the mixes of maple, oak, and birch, to name a few, that were in our forest.

Snow fell upon the treetops and layered the ground, crunching beneath my feet.

I wasn't alone, however. Dimitri and Gabriel were with me, and the mysterious lady too. As usual, Isaac, Julia, and Delilah were nowhere to be found.

The forest was quite pretty, with icicles adding a dramatic effect to the pine trees, and the snow crunching, along with the whistling of the wind, created a calming scene.

Red cardinals perched on the trees around us, adding more than the white and dark evergreen colors in the forest.

Suddenly, as I'm admiring a cardinal, I am dropped into the camp. Outside of the tents, just in the center.

No one is accompanying me, sadly, and the eeriness was keeping me wide-eyed, goosebumps crawling on my skin.

For a while, I just walked around, wishing I had a lighter, because the moon couldn't light the way around the camp.

I could barely see, but at least there was a little light from outside, but that's it.

My instinct was to go to the tents, see if anyone else was awake, but my body was revolting, just standing still.

It was like sleep paralysis, but no sleep paralysis demons, to my absolute delight.

Suddenly, I heard a scream. I didn't actually know where it came from, though. It sounded like it was everywhere.

I panicked. I decided to check up on everyone in the tents, but before I could, I was pulled back into the forest from earlier.

The birds were chirping happily in the trees as Gabriel, the lady, Dimitri, and I were trudging through the thick snow.

Snowflakes landed on my face as we advanced somewhere, I wasn't sure where, hell, I didn't even know where we were *currently!* The only thing I knew was that we were in a forest with a bunch of evergreen trees, with Red Cardinals and icicles decorating the trees like it was Christmas or something.

"Hey, Gabriel?" I asked.

"Yeah?" He responded, sounding slightly sad. "Are you alright?" I felt as though he may be depressed.

Not just his tone of voice, but how he walked, which had been that of someone quite determined, but now, he walked with his head down, his shoulders falling forward slightly. "Yeah, I'm fine." He responded in a monotone, looking back at the snow before us, and I just knew something was wrong.

I had no idea what was making him sad, but I was going to find out, one way or another. I turned to Dimitri, who seemed just as sad, but was doing a better job at hiding it.

"Hey, Dimitri, you don't look alright. Is everything okay?" I felt incredibly stupid asking him if he was okay *right after* saying he didn't look fine.

"Oh no, I'm fine, Livia." He smiled at me, and I just knew it was fake.

I do this with everyone else, too. I know *exactly* what's going on. They're trying to hide it to either convince themselves they actually *are* fine, they want to stay strong for the others, or they just don't wanna be an inconvenience. I know how it works, and yet, I struggle with doing it as well. Does it make me a hypocrite?

I mean, I think it's a bad thing, but I do it as well.

Also, I apparently give some pretty helpful advice, and I'm a pretty good "therapist" myself, but I don't take my own advice!

To make matters worse, people have told me it's kind of annoying, and they've accused me of being an "attention seeker."

We continued to make our way through the deep snow, the cardinals continuing to sing, making me assume it was the morning.

It felt tranquil, just the three of us walking in a peaceful setting. I never thought it could be possible, before or after this bullshit.

This couldn't even be possible *during* the bullshit happening right now.

I was about to ask where we were, but then the sound of distant gunshots woke me up.

Chapter 11:

When the gunshots woke me, I inhaled deeply, but nothing too crazy really happened. Julia wasn't in the tent, but personally, I just think that she might have gone for a walk or needed to go to the bathroom.

Delilah was sound asleep, and I didn't want to wake her, so I carefully and quietly headed out of the tent.

As I yawned, heading for the exit to get some early exercise in, I could spot someone running towards the entrance.

At first, I didn't recognize them, and sadly, no one else was awake, meaning if they were a bad person, then I would have to defend the camp on my own.

That was a scary thought, in my opinion, but to my surprise, it was Isaac.

"Isaac?" I squinted.

Isaac looked like he had a rough night. Hell, he was covered in scratches and bruises, like he fought a cat, and, spoiler alert, the cat won.

"What happened to you?" I asked, quickly taking notice of the injuries as well as his panicked face, as though he had witnessed something disturbing.

"I-I'm not sure if y-you'd like to kn-know…" Isaac stuttered, grabbing at his arm, wincing at the pain.

"No, I think I would…" I gave him a suspicious look, feeling a little nervous about what had happened to him.

"Well…who's awake?" Isaac asked, looking around the camp, arms crossed weakly. "No one. Just us. I think Julia went on a walk or something, though." I responded, but strangely, when I mentioned Julia, his eyes slightly changed. "Umm…Julia's…gone." I laughed.

"I'm serious. I can take you to her."

"You're joking, right?"

"No."

I stare at him, a broken boy, telling me that Julia was dead. He *had* to be *joking,* right? There was *no way* she was dead.

"Show me the proof…" I whispered, my voice breaking.

Isaac led me through the woods, and all I could hope was that it was a prank. It *had* to be a *terrible* joke they were doing.

My vision blurred when I saw her. The largest lump in my throat materialized as I laid my eyes over her body, which was pinned to a tree.

"This can't be real..." All the words I could form.

She was too young. She was too innocent. She hadn't even turned thirteen yet.

Tears poured down my face, and I collapsed to the forest floor, on my hands and knees.

"This *can't* be real...it just *can't*..."

"Livia...I'm sorry..." I could barely see Isaac due to the tears blinding me.

Mud started to get on my leggings, and at this point, I didn't care. I couldn't seem to take my eyes off of Julia's small, lifeless body hanging from the tree.

I could feel my heart thumping hard. The pain swayed me to stay on the ground, but I managed to get myself to stand up.

My body was unbalanced, but I got myself to Julia, and as I stared at her, fear had frozen onto her pale face.

I didn't want to continue looking at her, the immense pain she went through to end up like this, and it just haunted me.

However, I didn't want just to leave her here, as she couldn't just be a body, becoming anything else in this damn forest that will eventually burn.

The tears stung as they fell down my face.

"D-do you know w-who did this...?" I slowly turned to Isaac, who put his head down and shook it.

"Well, did you just discover it on its own, or did you witness everything?" My voice continued to crack, making my heart beat faster.

I was sure that he was going to respond that he just found it, trying to get energy out, and we didn't even know who *would* do this. "I actually saw a shadowy figure, killing her, but before I could do anything, she had already pinned Julia to the tree and run off into the woods. It was *very* dark so that I couldn't recognize anyone, but Julia's shirt made it obvious, since it was still a little white, though there was also blood and dirt on it." Isaac's voice broke a couple of times as well; his voice was also very shaky as he described what he had witnessed.

"I *will* find out who's responsible!" I promised.

It may have seemed that I was promising myself, or Isaac, but deep down, it was a promise to Julia.

To make sure she received the justice she deserved.

"I didn't even get to apologize to her for what happened last night…" Isaac whispered, tears flowing down his face as well.

"Should we tell the others, though?" I asked. It was a stupid question, but it might actually be a good question to ask, because of Gabriel. "I'm not sure. On one hand, Gabriel would be crushed, but if they found out we were lying-" "But what if we found a way to make it so that it would look like we *all* discovered it?" I was smiling, but my eyes made it known that I was probably losing it.

"You know what? Maybe we *should* tell them. I've seen the movies. Their friends get angry with them whenever they keep a big secret like that." Isaac mentioned, sniffling and still crying.

I nodded, sniffling too, and I delicately unpinned Julia's cold body, and Isaac carried her legs as I carried her top half.

As we returned to the camp, my tears stained the ground, which could technically lead anybody to the camp, but at this point, I just *don't* care.

Clouds had covered the sky, and as the sky darkened, and rain was starting to fall upon the earth, I hoped nothing would strike us.

Julia's body wasn't that heavy, I mean, she's literally the size of a ten-year-old.

I cried even harder, but not of sadness. Just anger.

How could anyone *do* this? It was heartless, like a psychopath's level of heartlessness.

The rain may be even more convenient, because it washes out our footprints, and will sink into the ground, along with the tears of Isaac and me.

Maybe, if the forest ever grows back, the water from the rain and our tears could help renew the forest if the soldiers actually burn it.

We reached the camp, and I could see Delilah and Dimitri talking by the campfire. Gabriel wasn't in our line of sight, but he was definitely either in the tent or in the bathroom area.

"Hey guys! Where've…you…. been…?" Dimitri waved, but when he saw the body, he trailed off.

"It's…where's Gabriel? He needs to know immediately." I said, my face radiating anger, but tears falling from my face like waterfalls. "Hey, I heard my name?" He came out of the bathroom area, but when he saw the body, his smile faded.

"Who is that? I can't see well." Delilah squinted as Gabriel nodded concerningly in response.

"Gabriel…" I said weakly, "It's…Julia…"

Gabriel laughed, sending shivers down my spine. I could tell everyone else was confused and slightly scared.

"No….no no no…" Gabriel's hand came off his face, and his eyes were a shade of red I couldn't describe other than just pure red.

"She *can't* be dead…" Gabriel whispered, tears flowing down his face as he smiled. I'm not sure if I was shrinking or he was growing larger, but something like that was happening as he approached Isaac and me, carrying Julia's body, which for some reason seemed to get heavier.

"*That can't possibly be her,*" Gabriel spoke through gritted teeth.

Isaac and I maneuvered ourselves, as well as Julia herself, into a way for Gabriel to see and confirm that the body in front of him was, in fact, Julia.

I wished it wasn't true either, but we had to at least all *know* that Julia is dead, so we can all find out what to do about this.

I doubted we were gonna try to *revive* her or some dumb supernatural shit like that, but there could be a chance that we are so rock-bottom, or even trapped in its basement, that we'd actually go to the extremes to deal with the feelings.

He gazed at the body for only about 2 minutes, but time seemed to have slowed down, making it seem like 2 hours.

"How…dare…you kill her!" He lunged at me, his hands wrapping around my throat.

I yelped, hoping someone would stop him, but everyone was too shocked to move. I couldn't blame them.

His hands were significantly larger than mine, making it extremely difficult to get them off of me.

For a split second, I could see someone else choking me, and not Gabriel; I blinked through the tears that were swelling up in my eyes due to the pain I felt.

As I suffocated, my lungs began to burn. I gasped, trying to breathe on instinct, but I couldn't.

"P-please st-stop…" I managed to spit out as I began to accept my fate of dying.

I closed my eyes, preparing for the sweet release of death, so that I could actually be free from the pain.

Suddenly, I felt myself being let go of. *Did I die?* I wondered as I felt myself going a little limp, falling somewhere, still not sure where, but I didn't open my eyes.

I didn't *want to.* I'm not sure what I landed on, but it felt like arms. *Did my body fall into someone's arms? Am I about to die?* I started to panic.

Actually, I kind of *wanted* to die, at least *then* I wouldn't have to worry about the soldiers, or the forest burning, or if any of my friends were secretly planning to kill me or not. I think my body was placed somewhere. I could hear everyone, which was probably a good sign, or maybe not.

Is this really *what it's like to die?* I wondered, starting to go numb.

"Please don't die…" I could hear someone pleading; I could identify Dimitri's voice.

Should I fight it? Should I resist the urges? Time was of the essence, as the voices were starting to fade away.

No. They seem to care about me, plus Julia already died, so they don't need to mourn two people.

Before I could do anything to try to stay alive, I felt it.

Something or someone was doing something painful, but it was keeping me from dying, so I was happy, I guess.

My eyes opened, and I could see everyone surrounding me. I thought I could see the most familiar girl I have ever seen, her blonde hair blowing even without wind, her amber eyes glowing like sunlight, standing opposite where another girl, whose eyes were like icicles, her blonde hair shorter and messier, was standing, but I was probably hallucinating, because she seemed to glitch out, like this was…something… It was a little hard to breathe, but everyone started to cry tears of joy, I assumed, as they saw me coming back to life somehow. A pretty boy's face, with silvery blue eyes, calming and sweet, his smile big and bright, was probably what made me smile then. I couldn't sit up, but it felt nice to be close to him.

That was when the pain hit. My eyes widened, and I opened my mouth to express said pain, but nothing came out.

I could see an older boy in the corner, clearly distressed. I wanted to go to him. I wanted to apologize for it all. I don't even know what had sparked that, but I *needed* to at least *talk* to him.

There wasn't any way I could get up right now. The pain urged me to stay down, but I was desperate to get to that guy.

I wondered if any of the people surrounding me would oppose me if I were to just go for it and go to the guy in the corner to apologize.

They *have* to know me, right? They look a little familiar, but I'm still skeptical.

I'm just gonna go for it. No matter what pain I'll endure.

I sat up, but immediately fell back down, to which the pretty boy caught me and set me down gently.

"No, you can't get up right now. You need to heal. Please." His eyes screamed for me to listen and just lie there.

But they don't need to worry about me. They could help the older boy in the corner. He probably needs more support than I do.

I opened my mouth again, hoping actually to say something, but nothing came out, frustrating me.

The girl, as well as a different boy, walked away, looking satisfied.

However, the boy I seem to be mentally swooning over for some reason stayed, which made me feel better, but also worse.

Shouldn't they be worrying about the older boy in the corner right now? Especially the girl and boy who had walked away, shouldn't they be comforting him and asking what's wrong?

It all confused me, and along with the confusion came aggravation. They should also be helping the boy in the corner! Why aren't they helping him?

The questions I had couldn't even reach them, because for some dumb reason, I can't seem to talk!

Why, though? Was my biggest question.

Why was any of this happening? Another question was our location.

I couldn't see any sky because of a tarp, but out of the corner of my eye, I could see trees, meaning we were away from humans, but why?

I was infinitely confused about the reasoning for our strange whereabouts, but perhaps I could guess by trying to find memories.

Maybe I could find out something important too. Like the names of these people! I know who they are, but what are their names? I also needed to find out why the older boy in the corner was sad. I didn't just want to find out what was wrong; I needed to apologize to him. I'm not sure why, but I have the feeling that I owe him an apology.

Chapter 12:

According to Dimitri, the boy I had been swooning over, it's lunchtime. I'm not sure how I can eat while I'm "healing," and also how I can eat when I have to talk to the guy in the corner, who hasn't moved at all.

I'm starting to get concerned for his well-being, and I think I have a plan to get some information out of Dimitri, at least, because he seems to be the one who's most dedicated to making sure I'm healing fine.

So far, nodding and shaking my head has worked whenever it comes to communication, as well as gesturing towards something and giving a confused look, which will then make him proceed to inform me about whatever I was confused about.

Now is the time I can try to get any information about the older boy in the dark corner.

When Dimitri walked over to me, I knew I had to be smart about this. He gently sat me up, but before I could do anything, I saw flashes.

Someone held me by the neck. What confused me the most was the face. The face was a little hazy, but it was constantly switching from one haze to a different haze.

I blinked, and Dimitri was inspecting me, making sure I was alright.

"You, okay?" He asked, and I nodded, blushing at how close he was. He blushed as well, and we immediately tried to shake that off.

"Do you have any more questions?" He gazed at me, seeming eager to answer anything, and I knew this was my chance.

I gestured towards the dark corner, where an older boy, about fifteen, maybe, was just sitting, looking as though something terrible had happened.

"Oh," Dimitri uttered, his eyes widening as he seemed hesitant to answer.

"Well…that's..G-Gabriel. He…um…he…" The boy trailed off, frantic to find an answer.

I wondered why he was scared of telling me about Gabriel. It may be hard to breathe, and I can't speak for some reason, but I wanted to help Gabriel in any way I could.

Both boys seemed to be distressed, and I just gave up on getting information out of Dimitri, so as he paced, I slowly and carefully tried to stand up.

I stumbled, and Dimitri stabilized me, trying to get me to sit back down again.

"You have to heal, you're not in a position to be walking around!" He pleaded as I made my way to Gabriel.

"Oh…oh god." He said when he realized what I was trying to do.

"Please don't do anything drastic. I'm not sure if you blame him or not, but what I know of you, this is *definitely* not what you do. If anything, you'd just give him the silent treatment, like what you did with Delilah." Dimitri struggled to get me back, even though he seemed significantly stronger than I was.

Once I reached Gabriel, I tapped him on the shoulder, ignoring the immense pain in my chest.

Gabriel turned around slowly, but when he saw who I was, his eyes widened. After a second, they returned to the mix of emotionless and depressed they were for the split-second he didn't see me.

"I get it if you want to get me back or something, but if you do anything, just make it quick and painless, even though I don't exactly deserve that." His eyes gazed at me, tears starting to form in his eyes.

I gave him a look of confusion. Why did Dimitri, along with Gabriel, talk about something Gabriel had done?

It was baffling, and when Gabriel realized I didn't know what he was talking about, he relaxed, "So…does that mean you forgive me?" He asked, a hint of excitement in his voice.

I nodded slowly, still confused about what he was speaking of. I looked behind me, and Dimitri also seemed to relax.

I tried thinking of a way to communicate with actual words, but I doubted they had paper.

Searching for said paper, Dimitri and Gabriel stared at me in confusion, which was too bad for them, because they couldn't help me right now.

Finally, I had found the paper, and then I searched for a pencil or something, and thankfully, after about five minutes of searching, I had found one.

I walked back to Dimitri and Gabriel, trying to explain what I wanted to know. "I have just one question: What the hell did Gabriel do?"

"Well," Dimitri started, "he kind of..." "I almost killed you." Gabriel looked at the ground, regretful. "I'm very sorry, Livia..." his voice cracked, and he was not meeting my gaze.

"It's alright, Gabriel. I just hope you are alright."

I smiled at him as he glanced back at me, and I held my hand out, and he took it.

The pain I felt then was almost unbearable, but it'll be alright.

The other girl, I assumed was Delilah, and the other boy, whose name I found out was Isaac, walked over to us, smiling at our reconnection.

"So, what's lunch again?" Delilah asked Dimitri, who smiled towards me.

"It's fish and berries," he responded, gesturing towards Gabriel, who nodded.

"I'll start the fire."

Dimitri led me back to the log he had made me sit up against. I didn't resist this time, however.

I observed Gabriel as he cooked the fish, and then the flashes came again. This time, Gabriel's face was one of the interchanging faces of haze in the chokehold.

I then understood what Gabriel had meant when he said that he had 'almost killed me.'

Thankfully, no one noticed me in the trance, so no one had to worry.

"Hey, Livia, could you make sure the bugs don't get to the berries? Thanks!" Gabriel handed me a bucket full of various berries.

As I stared at them, resisting the urge to eat them, I wondered why we were in the forest.

Oh well, one day, I'll probably find out, and by then, I'll hopefully be able to talk again, so I won't have to communicate with paper.

***

It has been about three days, and I have just woken up. I've figured out what day it is today! It's Thursday, August 28, 2025.

We are living in the woods near the school, and it is currently World War III. Even better, there are soldiers invading; however, we're not sure where they're from. Certainly not from the U.S., but the bigger question was why they were seemingly after us.

What about the rest of the country? I thought, shivering, *is it also overrun? Is it destroyed?*

I can only believe it is, but also, where the hell are the other adults? I haven't seen any since our last encounter with the soldiers. However, there was an explanation that haunted me a little. *Drafted. They were probably drafted into this damn war.*

I looked over, and Delilah was still asleep. An empty sleeping bag was between the two of us.

It was Julia's. Today, we were finally going to have a funeral. I realized that when I woke up a few days ago, I saw her, but when she glitched and disappeared, it was most likely her ghost, and I probably *wasn't* hallucinating.

As I exited the tent, my ribs feeling better but still hurting a little bit, I glanced over at Gabriel, who was sitting on a log; no one else was awake.

I sat beside him, hoping to comfort him. He was staring into the distance, and I couldn't blame him.

Someone had brutally murdered his little sister and pinned her body to a goddamn tree!

After what was most likely thirty minutes, but felt like thirty hours, Dimitri walked out, looking melancholy as well.

Isaac and Delilah came out and carried the body to a hole we had dug yesterday. The two carefully placed the young girl's body in the hole, and Gabriel stood before the hole, about to give a speech.

"Julia Alexa Lorelei-Leonardo was two when her parents and sister died in a fire caused by her older brother, who ended up running away as Julia went into foster care."

The rest of us shed some tears as Gabriel spoke, clearly trying not to cry, but was sniffling and having slight voice cracks. "Julia spent four years in foster care until my family came along, and I met her for the first time. She was optimistic, even though she had been through so much pain, even in foster care. I could see the bruises on her arms as she tried hiding them. Many foster kids would pick on her. My family ended up adopting her, and Julia grew up with me.”

The tears were basically attacking Gabriel now, and he wasn’t doing a good job keeping them at bay.

“I defended her from that point on. I refused to let anything bad happen to her. During the pandemic, I comforted her whenever she got COVID-19. She’d help me through it as well. After the pandemic, she’d still help me cope with anything.”

Gabriel broke down into tears, which was strangely contagious, as the rest of us broke down as well.

“Anyways…” Gabriel sniffed, “When we heard about World War III, she was scared, but I promised her that I wouldn’t leave her side. Delilah found us after I killed someone who was trying to hurt Julia. We then stayed with her and Isaac, and sadly, I wasn’t able to protect her from…D-the *knife,* as well as *this.*” Gabriel started to hyperventilate, and I ran to him immediately to keep him from just spontaneously combusting.

Once he was able to breathe more slowly and heavily, I helped him walk over to where the others were, and Dimitri walked over to where Gabriel was.

“I would just like to say that Julia was one of the only people who really saw the better side of things during these shitty times, and I believe she’s in a better place now, and won’t have to deal with any more pain or trauma.” Dimitri stepped away from the grave, and Isaac went up next.

“Julia, if you can hear me, I wish I could have apologized for what I said to you four days ago. I shouldn’t have snapped at you, even if I was angry at the others.”

I felt moved by his words, as the tears weren’t just rolling down his face, but resembled literal waterfalls as he spoke.

Delilah hesitantly walked towards where Isaac was standing, and hesitated to speak for a few seconds.

“Well, Julia was an amazing person to be around. Even though we’re living in a world of a terrible state, she was someone who could light up as though nothing bad was happening, or would never happen. I thank you, Julia, for being a beacon of happiness in this depressive world.”

Delilah smiled bittersweetly, still sniffling, and I knew there were no words spoken to show how amazing Julia was. We all buried her, and Gabriel carved the words on a large rock:

Here Lies Julia Alexa Lorelei-Leonardo

Beloved By Many And Didn't Deserve Death

Rest In Peace, Lil Sis

After Gabriel finished the makeshift headstone, he laid it in perfect view for whoever was to pass by.

Gabriel seemed too depressed to cook, so I did, because personally, I was hungry, and maybe they would be hungry too.

I slowly cooked some food, because I think it was closer to lunch than it was to breakfast, as we were all sleeping in, plus how long it took for us to get the funeral running.

After I finished the berries, the others came out, smelling how delicious it was. I passed bowls out to each of them, and I accidentally filled more bowls than necessary.

I left the extra bowl out for Julia, even though she couldn't eat it.

We ate in silence, obviously, I mean, what would we talk about? The latest football game?

Personally, it would be hilarious if football continued during World War III. I mean, Delilah had been talking about football in her sleep for some reason, but whatever.

Gabriel was the first to leave, after eating, and he retreated into the boys' tent, where I assumed he was going to cry.

I was still at least halfway until I finished, and when thinking of Gabriel in there, mourning the loss of his sister, I couldn't imagine how much pain he was in.

I was almost about to cry more, but I breathed in and continued to eat as the others finished one by one.

Eventually, I was alone. Just sitting on the log, eating jam, with a full bowl next to me, some fruit flies and other bugs starting to eat it in place of Julia.

I could imagine Julia here, eating happily with me, not dead, and smiling as much as before.

But then, as I could see her and was just reaching out towards me, a shadowy figure stabbed her with a knife, as they smiled menacingly.

I stared at them in disbelief. Who could look at a little girl and just kill her without mercy?

Someone is sick and twisted. That's who. I needed to find out who it was.

I walked over to Julia's grave and sat in front of it, starting to cry again. "I'm gonna find out who did this to you."

I sniffled.

"I promise."

Chapter 13:

Today was the day. I awoke to some gunshots, and thankfully, as always, they didn't sound close.

Delilah was still asleep, and I silently cheered. I needed everyone to be asleep so I could set the day off perfectly, and hope they think something suspicious is happening.

But, to make sure this is perfect, I stepped out of the tent and was greeted with some birds singing outside, but no one else was awake.

Nice. I thought, *Now I can get down to business.* I set up a small fire to make breakfast.

The baby flames reached out for me, as though I were the mother, and I just smiled.

It was hilarious what the mind can perceive as similar to.

However, as I quickly made breakfast, hoping no one would wake up, I needed to narrow down the suspects.

Who would be capable of killing Julia? The possibilities could seem endless, but I have a sneaking suspicion it was someone among us.

Gabriel? No, he was too heartbroken when he realized. I mean, he literally tried to kill me because he thought I did it.

Personally, it wasn't really the worst reaction, as a lot of people would be clouded by grief and heartbreak.

Dimitri? I immediately slapped myself. I wasn't sure why until I realized what I had thought of. *No motive, and also, he would never do that to* Julia *of all people.*

What about Isaac? Everything clicked. It was definitely *possible. Wait, it makes so much goddamn sense because he was out there* alone. *And he had yelled at her the night of her killing.*

My mind was filled with Isaac's face, his eyes turning red, and horns growing from his head.

What the hell is happening? I thought as I tried to think of something else.

Flashes. And then the glitchy face of Gabriel and whoever the other person was, still strangling me, and then, I was warped back to reality, where Julia stood in the entrance of the encampment, frowning.

"Julia?" I called to her, but as I ran to her, she just disappeared.

Glitched out of the world, as though she had teleported somewhere far away.

I was confused, but shook it off, as it was probably just another hallucination, like before.

Returning to the fire where breakfast was finishing up, my mouth watered at the sight of it.

Once the rest of the breakfast had finished, I knew it was time. I ran to the girls' tent and stood beside Delilah.

"Wake up," I stated, tapping her on the head gently.

"Why?" She replied, half asleep.

"Because I made breakfast, and it better not be wasted during a war," I whispered, getting louder and sassier.

"One, fine," she groaned, "and two, language. It may be a war, but we shouldn't resort to that language."

"Gabriel uses it all the damn time…" I muttered under my breath, rolling my eyes.

As I sprinted to the boys' tent, Delilah sat at the log, impatient.

"Hey, people! I made breakfast, so get out of here before it becomes cold!" I yelled, softly enough for no one outside of the camp to hear, but loud enough for the boys.

I could hear their groggy noises and yawns as they emerged from the tent. I smiled as everyone took a seat on the log.

"Thank you," I said, and then Dimitri stood up, surprised.

"You can speak again!" His eyes widened, and he seemed quite excited about that.

"Oh yeah." I realized.

I hadn't noticed, and I didn't know if that was a good thing or a bad thing. Whatever. "Wow, I actually hadn't noticed that," Delilah admitted, Isaac and Gabriel nodding in agreement.

"Well, it's still an amazing achievement," Dimitri stated, and I felt my body temperature heating up rapidly.

My face burned as I tried not to smile, and the blush on my face was probably one of the most obvious things someone could see. I passed out plates of breakfast to keep myself from blushing anymore, and we ate. "So,

I just wanted to know if I could propose an idea of what to do today?" I asked, hoping they would allow me to present my thoughts. "Um, we need to get more information about the soldiers, but sure?" Gabriel shrugged, giving me the ok.

"So, I was thinking. Why would someone murder a random child in the forest? It didn't really make sense to assume it was a random person, so I was wondering, what if it was one of us?" I shrugged as I finished.

I was met with gasps from at least Isaac, maybe Delilah, but I wasn't really sure. "Why would it be someone in our group?"

Delilah asked, scoffing a little.

"Because of certain events I remember causing the perfect motivations for the murder." I proudly replied, confident that I was doing pretty well.

"I mean, it *would* make a lot more sense if it were one of us…" Dimitri spoke softly.

See, he gets it! I thought as the others were considering the idea.

"Hypothetically, if it *were* someone in our group, what would these 'motivations' you speak of be?" Gabriel asked, raising an eyebrow.

"I have an idea of who it could be, and their motivation lines up with the memories, as well as the fact that they probably think it 'couldn't be them' because of their, say, *relationship* with them!" I laughed, feeling as though I were a detective in some spy movie or something.

"Wow," Delilah said, completely shocked.

"So, who do you think it is?" Isaac asked.

"That's so strange, so eager to see who I think it is? Well, you're in for a damn surprise!" I dramatically announced, about to knock their socks off!

"¡Isaac Leañdro Morrigan! I believe *you* are the culprit in the murder of Julia Lorelei-Leonardo!"

Everyone gasped and immediately turned to him as his face morphed into a bright red cherry, sweat rolling off his face rapidly in large cascades. I was onto him now. I would avenge Julia and make sure no one else close to me dies. And that was a damn promise.

Chapter 14:

"Why me?!" The young man I used to hang out with every day exclaimed, seemingly "shocked" that I would even accuse him.

He was obviously a prime suspect as he was the one to initially see her get killed, as well as "find" the body.

It was pretty questionable and kind of suspicious.

"Okay, let's back up here." Dimitri stood up, confused.

"What?" I turned to Dimitri.

"I mean, what evidence do you have to come to that conclusion?" He asked, and I felt weird as he spoke.

"Okay, first of all, you do realize that you sound weird spitting out those big words, like evidence and conclusion." I narrowed my eyes at him as he looked away sheepishly, blushing. "*Second,*" I continued, "this man *says* he saw *someone else* killing her, not having a clear description of whomever it was, which technically makes sense because it was nighttime, but he doesn't even know the

murder weapon!"

I relished the look on his face. I had figured it out. Everyone was definitely surprised. Dimitri and Delilah seemed not to want to believe it, but Gabriel was definitely affected by it a ton.

"So, Isaac?" I asked, hoping he would confess immediately.

"It's not me! I swear!" He pleaded, it made me feel bad, but I couldn't let anybody see that. "Well, where was everyone that night?" Dimitri asked.

I already knew where everybody was that night after extensive research from yesterday, but let's see who's gonna lie.

"I was in the tent sleeping after…the big argument," Delilah informed. Checks out, she's telling the truth.

"I know Isaac was outside as the rest of us were asleep that night…" Gabriel muttered, tears threatening to escape his eyes.

"What about you, Isaac?" Dimitri asked. "I was outside, walking, trying to get myself together, and after wandering the forest for a few hours, and mind you, by the time I had stormed off, it was already dark, I saw a shadowy figure, who now that I think about it looked a lot like Delilah, brutally killed Julia, and I didn't know how to react." Isaac kept turning his eyes towards Delilah in a glare.

"But Delilah was in the camp the whole night!" I responded, "There isn't any evidence actually pointing towards Delilah being the killer." "I hate to break it to you, Isaac, but a lot of evidence is actually pointing to you being the murderer of Julia." Dimitri sighed, disappointed.

"No, I swear to God, and I swear on my life that it's not me!" Isaac was crying now. "Wait, what do we do with him?" I asked, not actually thinking about it this far.

"We should kill him. For Julia." Gabriel's voice broke as he spoke.

"Is that the best idea?" I countered.

Killing? I mean, if it could be justified because of Julia, but killing was immoral! It's not like I'm afraid of the legality, more the morality of the "justified murder" to get revenge.

But would it *really* be *that* bad? Was it too immoral? Or was it *actually* justifiable? Maybe it's a little *much*, so we should probably think of something else.

"I have a better idea," Dimitri announced. "W-what is it?" Isaac stuttered, terrified of what we were going to do to him.

"How about instead of murdering him in cold blood, we just kick him back into the forest where he cannot come back at all?"

Oh. Was it better than just dying? I mean, he wouldn't have *anything* or *anyone*! He would be exposed to the dangers of being alone and have a big chance of being eaten by a bunch of coyotes or something.

Personally, I would rather die than do that. And that's coming from *me*!

"Um. Could I actually take the dying option, please? I'd like to be dead rather than being alone in the woods." Isaac was shrinking as he asked.

"No. You will be alone in the woods, and we don't give a shit about whatever you do as long as it doesn't involve us at all." Dimitri said firmly.

"Could I at least take my sleeping bag?" He asked.

"Sure. But I'll be watching you closely to make sure that's all you have." Dimitri responded, following Isaac into the boys' tent.

What is happening? I had no idea. I just walked to the log and sat down, contemplating whatever the hell I was doing.

You know, sometimes you just wonder what the hell is happening and why you exist, etc. I'm still not sure why I ask myself those questions, because I never know the answer.

I'm not sure I ever *will* know the answer, but sometimes I just feel as though you just need to ask yourself what the hell you're doing with your life.

The trees may have blocked the majority of the light from the deadly laser we know as the sun, but it was still an eyesore to look outside because of how bright it was.

Thankfully, Isaac and Dimitri came out, and I will admit in my head that it was painful to see Isaac's tear-stained face leave, giving us the puppy eyes that made me feel horrible. I will *never* tell anyone.

As he left, I felt a piece of my heart disintegrating and blowing away in the morning breeze.

Something felt a little wrong with just kicking him out and even labeling him as the guilty one.

But all the evidence pointed to him being Julia's killer, so it *had* to be him, right?

Was it normal to feel bad about enforcing the right thing on the one who was obviously wrong?

Everything swirled in my brain as I watched Isaac disappear among the trees into the future.

I *do* think it *might* have been better than killing him, but only because at least maybe he'll survive, and I could apologize.

I don't think it was him anymore, but he probably was…

I DON'T KNOW! IT'S SO FRUSTRATING! IS IT NORMAL FOR IT TO BE SO HARD?!

I don't even know what's stopping me from just running off by myself and either just begging for death to come and get me so I don't get driven to insanity, or just doing it myself.

Maybe it was Dimitri and his grief. I couldn't do that to him, and I didn't need Gabriel to be more depressed than he already is.

Yeah, I shouldn't hurt them more than they are already broken. Plus Delilah. I'm not sure how she'd react, but she'd probably get driven to insanity herself.

She'd be the only girl in the group, and even though I don't "act like a lady" in her eyes, she'd still want me around because she can't just be the only girl in the group.

That wouldn't be very nice of me. In fact, it was quite the selfish thought.

Chapter 15:

First day without Isaac. I still feel shitty, but my idea could work.

"Hey Delilah?" I asked, hoping I could retrieve some information.

"Yeah?" She turned to me.

"So, you know how you and Gabriel would leave creepy messages all over town during the beginning of this shit?"

"Yeah? Also, quit it with the language." She corrected me, which was honestly starting to piss me off too much, but I couldn't let her know.

"Okay, but anyways, did you and Gabriel ever leave a name or something for people to refer to your mysterious people as…or something?" "Oh," Delilah looked a little puzzled, but figured out what I meant quickly, "we actually *did* leave a name! I think it was 'Fire and Ice', maybe?"

"That's so cool! But who was fire and who was ice?" I inquired, already having theories. "I was the ice, and Gabriel was the fire." Delilah smiled, and for some reason, it just made me shiver.

Thankfully, Delilah didn't notice that I shivered, so I just did my goodbyes and walked somewhere else.

I should go outside to find Isaac now. I thought. *I should say I'm gonna find some more food. We're pretty much out of berries, so I should get some more.*

I knew I needed to see at least if Isaac's alive, and when I do, I could sneak him some more supplies to make sure he doesn't die. "Hey, I'm gonna go get some berries!" I called out to everyone as I hung the basket on my wrist.

"Do you want anyone to go with you?" Gabriel yelled in response.

"No, I'm good!" I shouted, hoping no one would jeopardize my mission.

"Okay! Good luck out there!" Gabriel responded, making me smile a little. They had actually bought it.

I hid a couple of knives in the basket. Isaac should be able to use these, right? He could hunt with them, fight maybe?

No matter what he uses them for, he'll definitely be able to survive longer. I just hope he's not already dead, because I can already expect what I will do.

"Isaac?" I called out once I was far enough away from the camp.

Personally, I didn't feel good in the woods right now, and I'm almost regretting going alone.

Shit. If something, or worse, some*one* jumps out of the trees, and since the air in the woods was dense, I can't run away without either tripping on a tree root or stopping to gasp for air.

My eyes darted around, inspecting the trees for any signs of threats. Nothing really seemed out of the ordinary, so I warily continued deeper into the forest.

I still couldn't shake the paranoia away, which pissed me off a little, but I needed to be sure of Isaac's survival.

The forest was starting to get darker, but there weren't any storms rolling in. It was just that there were no more clearings, and I would need to be more observant.

"Isaac?" I called out again, hoping for an answer.

"Livia?" I heard something behind me, but it wasn't a long distance.

I could see Isaac waving me over. I carefully made my way over back to him, making sure nothing fell out of the basket, and I didn't trip on a tree root.

"Are you a hallucination?" We had asked in unison.

"No, I don't think so…" Both of us responded to each other in unison, which was quite strange to me.

"I'm so happy you're alive!" I started to cry and then apologized, admitting that I started to have second thoughts.

"I could tell when you guys were deciding my fate." Isaac smiled. He seemed to forgive me, which was amazing in my opinion, but I'm not exactly sure if I deserve it.

"I brought you some knives to help you out here, for hunting, fighting, etc." I showed him the array of knives, and his eyes might as well have had stars in them.

"Oh my god…" The only words Isaac could utter.

He gladly took the knives and placed them on his sleeping bag. His sleeping bag was in a little cave-ish area, near a brook.

Another perk about the location was that no one could get down there without risking the drop onto sharp rocks.

"You know, this is a pretty smart shelter." I admired how he's made this area his "home." "I only found it last night, and the lighter kept going out because of the rain," Isaac explained. "The lighter actually saved me from falling off the cliff. I safely got down and set up after making sure it was safe."

I'd be surprised that he could do any of the stuff he did if I weren't so unsurprised, because he had been this way in school.

One of the top five in the grade, I think he's number four, maybe number three. The top spot belonged to Sophia Saonn. *Wait. If Isaac isn't the killer, then who is?* I pondered, feeling overwhelmed. "Oh damn. I'm supposed to get berries for the others. They're probably wondering where I am. Oh no…" My eyes widened as I remembered what my excuse was.

"It'll be okay, Livia," Isaac instructed.

"Thanks…" I said, breathing a little steady, even though they probably *were* wondering where I was.

"You can go get the berries, but just say you got lost a little, and finally found some, and it took a little to get back," Isaac shouted as I started to climb the rocks, hoping I didn't fall.

"Oh, and if you wanna find me again, just follow the river to the cliff above us." "Ok!" I responded, hurrying back, hoping I was even going the right way.

Damn it. The trees seemed to work against me, but if I breathe slowly and deeply, I won't be as breathless.

I tried as I ran, which didn't work. I figured it wouldn't, but getting back to make sure no one's too suspicious was too important. My legs started to tire out, and I

immediately stopped running. It wasn't far; I could see the tarp, but as I gasped, I knew I needed to continue.

I needed to get those berries. There was a berry bush close by, so I forced my body to get up and move over there.

The berries were fresh, and thankfully, they weren't the poisonous ones, so we were safe. I took as many as I could, trying to hurry back.

Once all the fresh berries were in the basket, I made sure none dropped as I quickly made my way back to the camp.

"Hey, sorry if it took too long. Got sidetracked…" I placed the berries with the other food.

"What do you mean by 'I got sidetracked?' What happened?" Dimitri interrogated, concerned a lot more than I thought *anyone* would be.

"I'm fine! It's just-"

"Oh my god, you're bleeding from your neck!" He inspected, starting to panic.

"How?" I asked, my hand going to feel the spot where it was apparently bleeding, but he caught it and kept it away. "I'm gonna grab something for that."

"Don't touch it!" Dimitri said sharply, keeping my hand away, as I just sat on the log, confused.

How did I cut my neck? There wasn't anything sharp, and I didn't even feel anything. "Okay, this might sting, but understand that this is gonna clean your wound." He advised calmly, preparing for what he probably deemed "The worst."

The cleaning substance or whatever touched my neck. Was it secretly a knife? No. It didn't look like one.

I was sure I was being stabbed in the neck, but Dimitri held me in place so that I couldn't move away, and I desperately wanted to.

"I know it hurts, but trust me, you don't want it to get infected." His eyes were overflowing with worry and sadness.

Why sad though? Was it because of the wound? Was it because I seemed reckless and unfit to be out there alone?

I didn't want him to be sad, so I should tell him that, right?

"Please still allow me to go out there alone. I don't know how I got it, I swear!" I pleaded, hoping he would let me.

"But you could get hurt again, and judging by the state of your body after going out there…" "What?" I asked, but he shook his head.

After he cleaned the wound, he wrapped it in bandages, and since it was pretty close to my face, part of my face was in bandages. "There you go, but please refrain from going out there. Thankfully, the actual cut wasn't big enough for stitches, so we're good."

I thanked him and returned to the girls' tent, where Delilah was picking stuff out from under her nails with her knife.

Honestly, it was pretty grotesque and also highly dangerous, but if she thought it was good, then she could risk getting hurt.

I lay on my sleeping bag, trying to recall one time I was truly happy, but before all of this damn war stuff.

Probably when my fifth-grade class was undefeated in a kickball tournament during the last week of school that year.

We were the Gunter Geico Geckos, as G could be for the color green, my teacher, Mrs. Gunter, and geckos, so one of my friends, Nathan, suggested we call ourselves the Gunter Geico Geckos.

The day of the tournament, we all wore some kind of green shirt, and Nathan had brought these green bead necklaces with keychains on them with a picture of the Geico mascot wearing military attire to show we mean business.

I remember a kid named Michael taking his shirt and tying it into a weird-looking crop-top after one of the games we won.

Pretty much every class we destroyed cheered on the Sanders Spider-Monkeys, and a fun fact, Mr. Sanders was my 4th-grade teacher, but became a fifth-grade teacher the next year. We dominated everyone, but we didn't have time to face off against the other undefeated team, which was the Smith Superstars.

Fifth grade was an interesting year, now that I think about it. I mean, I went into Middle School, I learned about how the world worked due to actually understanding what the radio said, and learned about the LGBTQ+ community.

Plus, the war on the other side of the world or whatever. The kids took it a little too seriously, and I mean it.

Different groups were created, but anything that would unite certain groups would just be what side you were on.

I mean, a group led by one kid I had a crush on at the time, named Silas, declared war on a friend of mine, who was a little too fond of me, and sometimes I wonder if she actually *did* have a crush on me.

A rumor went around that we kissed, and I'm still trying to forget that, since it was very believable.

Betrayals and alliances occurred, and honestly, I'm happy that I moved away from that place, because so many strange things happened, and I couldn't handle the rumor, because it was probably true.

I don't know why, but I remember my other friend Amelia and me sitting on the curb talking about something when a boy fell face-first on the asphalt sidewalk, and nothing happened.

He didn't have a scratch or any skin peeling from the experience, and he just got up like it was nothing.

Personally, I would have at least *checked* to make sure I wasn't bleeding or anything, but maybe it's different for boys.

Perhaps boys aren't that worried about that stuff, at least that boy wasn't.

"Hey, you good, Livia?" Delilah peered over at me, still lost in thought, but snapped out of it. "Oh yeah, I'm okay. Just spacing out. Escapism, you know?"

Delilah nodded slowly and exited the tent, probably to check up on something or someone.

I continued to go through my memories, laughing internally.

The beginning of when this all started. I remember running. I remember feeling like I was being watched.

I wondered if any of the boys were out there, alive and well. The girls were probably all dead now, though.

Avery Marengo, however. She could survive. Maybe she's still out there. Maybe I could sneak out and try to find her.

I know some places she would go, and I could even try her house, too.

No. I'm not allowed to. Plus, I don't think it'll be easy, as well as the risk of the soldiers following me, leading them to the camp, and I don't wanna be responsible for that.

I *could* try to convince them to help track her down and ask her if she wanted to join our little group.

Wait. That would be replacing Isaac. I can't do that. Or maybe I could? I don't know anything anymore.

I think I'll just sleep and wait to deal with it. I mean, I haven't really felt rested at all during this bullshit.

I don't know if Delilah would care or not if I just took some time for sleep, so I could be ready for anything to come our way! Who knows at this point? Delilah's quite difficult to read, because she has different personalities with different people, but one trait in all of them is the same: her rudeness.

She does seem like she's changed, though, since I haven't heard any condescending comments or seen any side-eyes or dirty looks.

Maybe we'll actually survive this. Maybe we can wait it out and afterwards, hope we can start a better life, where we can be who we wanna be, as I doubt any of the kids in our grade will be around after this is over.

I'll still think of Avery Marengo and hope she's still alive and actually around somewhere in Brooklyn.

Chapter 16:

I was jolted awake by Delilah, who looked a little concerned.

"Wake up, damn it!"

"Fine. I'll steal my Nutella back some other time." I muttered as I got up and exited the tent behind Delilah.

On the log, eyes wide and angry, the scarf we used on Delilah was the only thing keeping her from talking. It was a girl.

Her seafoam-colored eyes were glaring at Delilah and me, and I could have sworn I'd seen those eyes before.

"Who is this?" I asked, there was something familiar about her, but I couldn't figure it out. "It's Avery Marengo," Delilah responded casually.

"Wait, what?!" I gasped, "At least take the scarf out!"

Delilah reluctantly, and looking a little annoyed, undid the scarf, and Avery immediately started insulting us.

"You BITCHES! WHY THE *ACTUAL* HELL

DID YOU DO *THAT* FOR?!" Avery glared at the two of us.

"I'm sorry, Avery. I didn't know you were in a state like this." I desperately didn't wanna die, and messing with Avery was a one-way ticket to hell or something, I don't know.

Avery's brown hair was incredibly short now. It used to be so long and lustrous, but I suppose when it comes to maneuvering through tight spaces or being chased, it would be smart to avoid long hair.

I'm such a hypocrite, since my hair's been long ever since I was little.

"I mean, you *did* come out of that tent, and weren't with her before, but why are you with her even now?" Avery asked.

"I don't know. Gabriel and-" I contemplated whether or not I should mention Julia. "It's okay, Livia. I saw the grave. I know about Julia." Avery said sympathetically.

"But they came across Delilah, and then Isaac found them, and then we all kind of just lived together until the soldiers found us."

Avery didn't seem surprised at the soldiers' part, but at how we all just decided to live together.

"And where is everyone else?" Avery asked. "BOYS, GET OUT HERE!" Delilah called out to them, and they groggily got out and gave her a dirty look.

However, once they saw Avery, their eyes widened to the point that they looked a little bit like cartoon characters when they see something unexpected.

"Avery?" Dimitri shook his head, not believing what he was seeing.

"Yep. I'm being interrogated or something, but I'm not totally sure. The bitch isn't that clear with it." Avery tried to shrug, but it looked weird to me. Delilah, on the other hand, was obviously trying to resist the urge to kill her.

"Who was the one who did this?" Gabriel asked, a little hint of frustration in his voice.

"It was Delilah Mortimer," Avery stated casually, as though this was a normal thing.

"I'm untying these," Gabriel muttered.

"What's wrong?" Delilah asked, annoyed.

"Do you know who he is?" Avery gestured towards Gabriel.

"No." Delilah rolled her eyes.

"We're cousins," Avery said flatly.

"Cool," I said.

"Wait. You said Isaac was part of your group. Where is he?" Avery looked around, trying to spot him.

"Um-" I was cut off.

"He's probably dead. But we convicted him for killing Julia, so we sent him out into the woods with just a lighter and a sleeping bag." Delilah explained proudly.

"Did he, though?" Avery pushed further. "All the evidence pointed to him, so he was obviously the killer, plus he had a motive." Delilah was on a roll with the summary, but Avery was stubborn, so she dug even deeper. "What was the motive?" She asked, smirking a little.

"We learned some information, and Isaac didn't agree with our plan for something, and when Julia agreed, he snapped at her and then ran into the woods, and so did Julia. Isaac was the only one who came back." Delilah smirked back at her.

Avery thought for a moment. I could feel sweat starting to form in my hands as I waited for her to speak.

What was she thinking about? The real killer? I still don't know who the killer is!

There isn't any motive for anybody but Isaac, and the evidence all points to him, too. Damn it. Not this worrying again. I need to breathe. Slowly and deeply.

"So, what if he wasn't *actually* the killer?" Avery pondered.

"Impossible. He *had* to be the killer." Delilah immediately retorted.

"But what if he wasn't?" Avery repeated.

"Again, everything points to him. Who else could it be?" Delilah was starting to get angry. I feared the worst. If they got into a fight, then it could escalate, and it would bring in the rest of the group, and maybe even reveal that I visited Isaac and gave him weapons. Maybe I could stop the fight right now to keep it from snowballing into a large avalanche or something.

"I have some ideas!" Avery exclaimed, and honestly, she might be able to help us out, and I don't have to worry that Isaac died.

"Oh, really? Who?" Delilah challenged. "It could be either of you. The other two wouldn't." Avery suggested.

"Why me?" Delilah and I asked in unison. "Well, for you, Livia, you don't really talk to anyone, and judging by how you didn't really want to speak of Julia, it means you two were quite close, and that would be the perfect alibi."

I was speechless. It was a genuinely good reason why it could be me. It's not, but Avery's really smart. I bet she's never been beaten at a mystery game.

"And for you, bitch-"

"DON'T CALL ME THAT, YOU BASTARD!"

Delilah screamed. I'm surprised my eardrums haven't *already* ruptured.

"Whatever," Avery sighed, "Anyways, it could be you, Delilah, because you don't seem bothered at the sight or the mention of Julia, which is a little strange. I assume you have a crush on Gabriel, so if he really only cared for Julia, it would make you spiral down a path to make sure you were the only one Gabriel paid any attention to." Avery gestured at Delilah. I think Delilah was speechless, too. I hadn't even *thought* for *one second* about these details.

Avery smirked at Delilah's expression, which looked quite horrifying, and I wouldn't wish for my worst enemy to see that face.

"Well, now it all comes down to the boys." Avery walked to the boys and brought them to the log.

"So basically, Livia could be the real killer because she has the perfect alibi of being really close with Julia," Delilah announced, pacing around the two of us.

"But Delilah could be the real killer because Julia was in the way of either or both relationships she had with Gabriel and Livia," Avery muttered, rolling her eyes.

The boys looked shocked to say the least, and I think they might have been more speechless than we.

"Wait!" I exclaimed. Avery turned to me, curious about what I had to say.

"The whole 'perfect alibi' thing was one of the pieces of evidence used against Isaac, and since Avery doesn't think it's Isaac, would it really be me?" I tried to persuade them not to think it's me.

"Well, it's one of you, but you could also be lying anyway." Avery accused.

"I have something to confess," I admitted

Chapter 17:

"I've been feeling shitty for accusing Isaac, and when I went out for berries, I took some knives and brought them to Isaac. It took me a while to find him, but shortly after we were trying to make ourselves feel better about the situation, I had to get back here, or else you guys would try to come find me." I was out of breath by the time I finished that sentence, and everyone was definitely not expecting that.

I don't blame them, though. They were thinking I was gonna confess to the crime I had "committed."

"I wasn't expecting that at all," Avery murmured, rethinking something.

"Why didn't you tell us?!" Delilah shrieked, her eyes flashing red for a second.

"I didn't want anyone telling me that Isaac was the one who killed Julia!" I responded, not at the same volume, but close.

"Delilah, you don't need to be so aggressive," Gabriel grunted, shooting her a dirty look. "Whatever," Delilah muttered under her breath as she rolled her eyes and crossed her arms, "Personally, I wouldn't be surprised if it were you or Avery!" Delilah pointed at me, and I just glared at her.

"You better not think it's Livia! She wouldn't!" Dimitri threatened, his eyes darkening. I definitely blushed deeply after he said that, and my body temperature rose as well. "Well, you don't know that! She could have been hiding her true self!" Delilah's words pierced my heart. A knife twisted as it surged deeper into my back.

"For three years?" Dimitri retorted, raising an eyebrow as the intensity of the argument escalated.

What if I walked away? I asked myself, *would they notice if I were to walk away?* The answer wasn't as straightforward as it may have seemed to me, but a second after I thought of it, I knew it was unpredictable.

Gabriel and Avery were just stuck watching Delilah and Dimitri fight, while I just walked away from it, and no one seemed to notice.

I felt quite mature. We were told as tiny children that it was the mature thing to do just to walk away.

The screams of insults between the two seemed more like toddlers fighting or even adults debating about something stupid.

I rolled my eyes as I retreated into the tent, hoping no one would notice, and my experiment would work.

The light from outside filtered a little bit, but most of the time we just used a small lantern to at least keep us from tripping over each other.

I kind of wished I had retreated to Isaac's cave instead of the tent. Their screaming was going to drive me insane at this point.

Maybe I should just stop them from arguing so we don't attract any unnecessary visitors.

They weren't going to stop, and personally, I wouldn't blame Gabriel and Avery for enjoying themselves threatening each other, but it was kind of getting annoying.

I wouldn't do it in a pick-me style. I wouldn't break them apart and start saying weird things like: "Oh my god! Look at me, this isn't you! Please!"

I would just tell them they are being annoying, and it would be amazing if you guys would either quit arguing like toddlers or be a little quieter because we don't know who else could possibly be in these woods.

Wait, I can't! I'll hurt someone's feelings. They'll get mad at me. I don't wanna make anyone angry, so maybe I should rephrase it?

Like: "You two aren't getting anywhere, and what you two are even debating over is incredibly stupid. Plus, you two screaming will probably attract something or someone we don't wanna have to deal with."

That might have just been the same, or maybe worse. I'm not totally sure, but I don't wanna be mean to either of them at the end of the day, so perhaps I should talk to Gabriel or Avery?

One of them could speak, and it would be like it was them, so they'll listen, especially if it's Gabriel.

I peeked out of the tent a little, and sure enough, they were all still distracted. I crept over to where Gabriel was and proceeded with the plan.

"Sure. I'll make sure they know the risks." Gabriel smiled at me, and that was something I felt as though was as rare as finding a four-leaf clover.

"Thanks!" I whisper-shouted for no reason. "LISTEN UP!" Gabriel announced, "You guys need to stop screaming. We don't need unnecessary visitors. *And* it isn't even going anywhere. The topic you two are even debating about is foolish!" Gabriel's expression was probably the main drive for anyone to listen to him, which I'm glad he doesn't abuse that power.

The two glared at each other as Gabriel and I sat them down. I could have sworn I had seen Dimitri flip off Delilah for a split second as I was navigating him to the log.

Gabriel stood up this time, and Avery reluctantly took his place on the log. "So, apparently, the *main* suspects are Delilah and Livia. We need to determine everything, and I'm pretty sure we had an eyewitness." I was intrigued by Gabriel's tone. It was as though he were a narrator for a murder mystery story.

"Wait," Delilah said, unimpressed, confused, and annoyed all at the same time, "what do you mean by 'had' a witness?"

"I mean, we had Isaac, and he technically was an eyewitness, and since Livia's found him, we could potentially beg for forgiveness and ask him for help." I think Gabriel was on autopilot mode then, but he had a point.

Isaac deserved an apology; hell, he deserved even more! I know he'll probably forgive Gabriel, but I'm not so sure about the other two.

"So, you guys kicked Isaac out because you thought he was the killer?" Avery asked. We all nodded. I hung my head down as I did, my hair getting in my face a little.

"But then you two didn't think he was, but it was already too late?" Avery pointed at Gabriel and me, and we nodded.

"And then you secretly found Isaac, and as you prepared to die, you shared the vital information that you knew where Isaac was, hoping to stay alive?"

She was good. I nodded slowly, trying to process it, and she might as well be a fortune teller or something like that because this girl was able to tell what had happened with only vague details.

"It's getting late, so maybe tomorrow we should look for Isaac?" Avery suggested, and it was quite agreeable, so I nodded.

Pretty much everyone went to their tents, but Avery stayed on the log.

"Hey, we have room!" I whisper-shouted to her, so I didn't wake anyone else up.

"No, no, it's alright. I'm good." Avery smiled, lying on the log.

Maybe she actually was comfortable, but it was a little weird to just sleep on a random log.

Chapter 18:

Gunshots have awoken me yet again, louder this time, and personally, it was like my own alarm clock because no one else would wake up to them.

Maybe I've been going crazy ever since this started, but perhaps something else has been going on.

Outside was bright this morning, and it was blinding compared to the shady camp.

Avery wasn't sleeping on the log, but doing something with the fire.

"Hey, Avery!" I called out, trying to smile, but it wasn't going for me.

"You need some help, but I don't think therapists exist during World War III!" She chuckled, smiling brokenly back at me. "The kids in our *grade* need help more than I do!" I laughed back.

It was true. They really *did* need help. Actually, scratch that, they need to be put in Arkham Asylum with the damn Joker!

That's how unhinged they are! Or…were. I'm not sure how many are actually dead, but Sophia Saonn, Alli Divas, and Molly Omitterres were the ones I know for sure are dead.

"Well, do you want some fish?" Avery offered.

"Sure! Where'd you get the fish?" I asked.

Did Avery get the fish from our stash of food? Did she already have some fish with her? "Oh, I had some food with me in a bag, and I actually found the bag this morning. I assume Delilah hid it, trying to keep me from it, but I found it." She smirked, letting out a small 'ha.' I gladly accepted the fish, taking a small bite to be sure it was cooked well. That fish, though, was the epitome of happiness then.

The juiciness and flavor of the fish almost made me fall to the ground. I think the fish was filled with some kind of love potion or something because my cheeks started to hurt as I beamed.

"You like it?" Avery snickered as she turned back to where some other fish were being prepared.

"Oh yes, I do," I muttered, my mouth watering as I tried to take another bite.

Drool escaped from me as more fish entered my mouth, and I wiped it away with my sleeve, trying not to drop the fish.

I needed to sit down, so I wobbly made my way to the log, where I felt amazing feelings.

I could never explain it perfectly, but I'm pretty sure I experienced true happiness for one of the first times since the beginning of this damn hellscape.

Gabriel exited the tent, and once he laid eyes on me, he looked horrified.

"I wanna ask, but I also don't." He stared intently, clearly weirded out.

"What? She really likes fish!" Avery smiled at him, shrugging.

"Seriously?" Gabriel said, dumbfounded.

He sat down on the log, a considerable distance away from me, and side-eyed the shit out of me, but I didn't really care, as this fish was better to pay attention to.

When Avery passed him a fish, he took one look at it and seemed to fall into the same trance I just escaped from.

The fish was quite delicious, so now, he can experience the happiness he's been needing.

"I bet you regret giving me weird looks now that you get to experience it, right?" I asked smugly.

"Uh..huh..?" He mumbled, drool dripping from his face onto his pants.

I tried to contain my laughter, but some giggles escaped, and it started to annoy Gabriel.

"Seriously. Stop laughing at me!"

"But you're being hilarious! Plus, you gave me weird looks, so I can technically laugh at you." Ha! Technicalities and psychology for the win!

Gabriel huffed, but continued to eat his fish, his eyes basically having hearts in them.

Delilah walked out and immediately turned around to go back to the tent, but I stopped her.

"Just because Gabriel looks ridiculous doesn't mean you should just go back to the tent. Plus, didn't you say that staying in the tent all day was lazy?" I was on a roll today!

Delilah rolled her eyes and walked to the log, sitting far away from Gabriel, and I couldn't blame her, as that was what Gabriel had done with me.

Dimitri was the last one to come out of the tents, and when he saw the state we were all in because of the fish, he broke down laughing.

"Hey!" Delilah shouted, clutching her fish in her fist as she stomped over to Dimitri, eyes narrowed.

"What?" He asked, wheezing from laughing too much.

"You can't laugh at us, since the fish has affected everyone!" Delilah waved the fish in his face, or tried to.

Delilah was significantly shorter than Dimitri, but she was the tallest girl in our group. Since she was shorter than him, it made the experience even funnier than her just hitting him with a fish.

Dimitri seemed to find this amusing as well, as his face was turning bright red from all the laughter he was clearly trying to suppress. "I said, quit laughing!" Delilah reprimanded, still waving the fish around.

As soon as she finished, we all started bursting into laughter, and Delilah's face scrunched up in a pout.

"What's the matter, Delilah? Mad you don't have any Authoritah over us?" Dimitri giggled. "Oh my god, you guys are the worst!" Delilah screamed and stormed off into the tent.

We all immediately stopped laughing, staring at the tent, hoping she'd come back out. I'm pretty sure we were all going to start laughing again when she came out to just troll her. I mean, it's World War III, but can't we have some fun? We *are* kids.

Delilah didn't come out. We heard some thrashing in there, as though she were attacking something, and I started getting concerned for her.

"Well," Avery broke the silence, "we can either figure out what we should do with Isaac and the murderer, or we could wait for Delilah to come back out to do it."

I advocated for us to get Delilah out here instead of waiting, and the others seemed to approve.

Yes! Finally! I thought, congratulating myself for being able to come up with something that others would agree to.

The thrashing had stopped, but something about getting Delilah out seemed quite terrifying.

"Hey, Delilah? We were gonna decide what to do, can you come out?" I asked, my eyes closed so I didn't have to gaze upon anything disturbing.

"Fine," Delilah replied flatly, pushing me away as she exited the tent.

Her eyes seemed more bloodshot than I remembered, which might be our fault, but I'm not sure I care. I mean, she's kind of a jerk sometimes.

"So…what do we do now?" Delilah asked sassily, clearly wanting to get it over with. "I propose a plan for us to be able to get the most done today, or at least be able to be productive," I announced, hoping no one would oppose, but I knew Delilah probably would.

"I think we should split up into two teams. One team will gather more information about the soldiers and their plan, while the other team goes on a mission to retrieve Isaac, as he's definitely not safe out there." I felt as though it

It was a pretty good plan, and thankfully, everyone seemed satisfied with it.

"But who would be on each team?" Delilah scoffed, changing expressions. She knew it was a good plan, but for some reason, she wanted to challenge it.

"That's simple!" I think I'm doing pretty well at biting back.

"Delilah, Avery, and I will retrieve Isaac while you two go see what's going on with the soldiers," I explained.

"You guys ready for this?" Avery asked, bracing herself and cracking her knuckles.

"As we'll ever be," I responded, smiling determinedly.

All of a sudden, I started breaking down laughing.

"I'm sorry, but I just referenced something, and it was absolutely hilarious." There were many pauses where I had to breathe and stop myself from laughing, which was starting to hurt. "You mean from that one show?" Delilah asked, as though it were preposterous that I would watch, or even know, of a show based on the events of Tangled.

"Well, I don't mind," Avery chimed in, "but we need to get going."

Delilah crossed her arms as I turned towards the exit, and we made our way to where Isaac was last seen.

The birds were watching us with a curious gaze as they gossiped with their fellow birds as we hiked.

"So, he was under a cliff?" Avery asked, breaking our silence, to my delight.

"Yeah. It was pretty smart." I replied, my eyes darting between the trees in case of an ambush. "Do you remember how long it took before you could find him?" Avery inquired, and I needed to think about it.

"Hmm. I'm not really sure." I responded, disappointed, "I didn't really pay attention to the time until I was already in a conversation with Isaac."

"Do you remember any important landmarks that could help us know we're going?"

"I know it was getting darker as I got deeper into the forest, but when you see a river, that's when we know we're probably really close."

Chapter 19:

We continued to walk, and our surroundings became harder and harder to really keep an eye on.

The clouds weren't the greatest help with the light either, and thunder was rolling in the distance.

"We need to do this fast." I said, "That thunder's not sounding promising."

I could see something in the distance, and I could hear some water running. "I think we're close." I started jogging towards the noise, trying to be mindful of where I step. The river was there, and the cliff was about thirty feet away, and I immediately propelled myself to the ledge and carefully dropped down into the little ravine where Isaac had been crashing in.

"Isaac?" I called out, hoping he would be there, and we could be halfway done at least.

There was no answer. *Maybe he's asleep?* I thought frantically, looking into the cave. There wasn't any light, and the sky was darkening, making this even harder than it needed to be.

"Shit. Does anyone have a lighter?" I asked the other two, hoping one of them would have one. I had forgotten mine back at the camp, which wasn't very smart of me, but hopefully one of them would have one.

"Yeah, here." Avery lit a match and handed it to me.

I grabbed a stick on the ground and lit it with the match. I would only hope I wouldn't burn the entire stick as I blew out the match and threw it onto the rocky floor.

Inside the cave, fabric and moss carpets lay across the floor, in layers. *To help with sleep.* I thought. It was actually really smart. As I looked around the little home, I saw a body lying unconscious, with clothes all over it.

"Isaac?" I handed Avery the make-shift torch as I crept in for a closer look.

As I got closer, I knew. It was Isaac, and he had come up with a way to keep himself from freezing in the night, which was getting colder.

"Isaac?" I tried waking him gently. His eyes flickered, and once he realized it was me, he smiled.

"I thought you said you'd be here sooner," Isaac smirked.

"Well, I'm here now!" I laughed, and Isaac sat up.

"Ahem." Avery cleared her throat, giving me a knowing glance.

"Oh yes, I'm sorry," I realized, "Avery and

Delilah is here, too."

"Oh, hey!" Isaac greeted the two, smiling.

"We should head back," Delilah finally spoke, "It's getting too dark, and the others are probably waiting for us."

Isaac immediately shot up from the ground, and we ran out to climb up from the small ravine.

The whole time back to the camp, we ran. I jogged for a bit, but I could still keep up at least.

"We should make sure to drink water after we get back," I mumbled, hoping we wouldn't be too preoccupied to ignore the dehydration. I could see the camp in the distance, and the thunder was getting louder and louder, and the sky was getting darker and darker.

Gabriel was in there, and so was Dimitri. Gabriel was pacing, probably because we took a little while.

"I'm so sorry for taking a while!" I gasped for breath, since I hadn't slowed down until we got back.

"Oh no, you're all fine, it's just, well, I think you guys need to sit down for this."

Gabrielwas trying to think of something. I wasn't sure what was on his mind, but it seemed bad.

"So, basically, I don't think we have much time left." Gabriel blurted.

"Wait, why?" Avery asked, surprised.

"Well," Gabriel started-

"The soldiers are going to burn down the forest to find whoever could be hiding here," Dimitri said bluntly.

Chapter 20:

"So, what you're saying is that this whole forest could be on fire any minute now?" Isaac cried, his eyes wide with fear.

"I estimate we have about ten minutes, give or take, based on the times of when they actually mentioned it and how fast we got back here," Gabriel remarked as we all started to panic.

I ran to get water because the dehydration was starting to hurt, and I could hear my heart thumping harder and faster.

I'm pretty sure I was hyperventilating, so I tried to keep myself from being overwhelmed with fear by breathing slowly and deeply, but it was pretty hard with the circumstances.

"What should we do?!" I mumbled, freaking out.

"Well, I know Isaac's not the biggest fan of leaving, but it's pretty much the only thing we can do if we don't wanna die," Dimitri mentioned.

"I don't even care at this point," Isaac commented.

"Well, we should probably pack some food and water." Avery also mentioned, and Gabriel nodded in agreement.

"We might not even have time for that…" Delilah informed.

"How so?" Dimitri questioned.

"Because I can see the fire starting," Delilah responded, pointing somewhere outside.

We rushed over to see if what Delilah had said was true, and I wish that she was wrong.

The light of the fire was spreading quickly, and we couldn't do any packing. We needed to make a break for it.

"We need to run," I muttered, just loud enough for the others to hear.

I started to run and turned back to see if the others were running too, and thankfully, they were.

I didn't know where to run, but I understood we needed to get as far away from that fire as we could, and we needed things from the camp.

Maybe if I just go in quickly, I could catch up to the others. I thought as I let the others pass me, and I turned back to the camp. "Livia! What are you doing?" Dimitri shouted, and the others slowed down.

"I need to grab you guys' water!" I yelled in response, hoping I could grab it.

"No! You'll die!"

It was too late. I was searching through the smoke-filled camp; it wasn't fully on fire, but the smoke was filling up in there, making it hard to see or breathe.

Thankfully, the water wasn't contaminated, so I grabbed as much as I could and started to try to run out of there as fast as I could without dropping anything.

To my surprise, I didn't die, and I made it back to the others, my vision starting to clear up, but then, the smoke started to make them water, and I couldn't see much again.

The fire was behind me; I could hear it. Thankfully, however, we were in a more rocky clearing, so as the camp behind us started to burn more, we watched from the less flammable area, losing a lot.

There were many things I held dear, and things I have lost, and this was something on both lists.

As I cried, seeing for myself the cruelty of humans, causing destruction such as this, to both the forest and the camp, I knew I would have to get over it.

I couldn't help myself, though. I wished I could scream, but it would alert the soldiers to where we were, so I could just silently cry.

Dimitri held me close. I appreciated that way more than I could ever describe. At least I hadn't forgotten Julia's gloves, as I was wearing them still. I could imagine Julia here right now, me holding her close as Dimitri was with me.

Julia really was like a little sister to me. Of all the people I miss from life, Julia's number one on that list.

The smoke was starting to get more intense. We needed to start breathing more shallowly and not breathe in too much smoke. I looked at Dimitri. He was staring intently, hatefully, into the fiery woods, the burning camp that would eventually be disintegrated into nothingness.

His pale eyes threatened the fire to stay away if the fire got even an inch closer; who knows what he'd do?

I don't even know what I was thinking, and it was definitely not the time, but I couldn't help myself.

I kissed Dimitri Raymond as he glared at the glowing mess in front of us.

"I'm sorry. I know it's a horrible time, but I couldn't help myself. I understand if you want to shove me into the fire." I couldn't even bring myself to look at him.

"I love you too, Livia." Dimitri smiled at me. "I just hate how this is happening."

"We all do," I responded, laying my head on his shoulders.

"I know, we need to get over this damn bullshit…"

"Well, even though there's a world war happening, we can still feel things like sadness and anger. We don't need to hide it all the time." I smiled at him, a tear rolling down my cheek.

"Okay," Dimitri responded, a smile forming on his face.

As we turned around, the others were gone, but their footprints were noticeable through the smoke.

We held hands as we dashed after them, hoping we weren't too far behind them. The fire was catching up fast, but at least I got everything out before we potentially die.

I mean, the good news about this was that we weren't too far behind them, as after about two or three minutes, we caught up to them.

The bad news, however, was that Avery was holding Gabriel back from Delilah, who was holding Isaac tightly, with her knife really close to his neck.

Chapter 21:

"Delilah…?" I couldn't believe it. But, I could?

"What the hell!?" Dimitri objected.

"If you don't want him to die, then don't come at me!" Delilah laughed.

She glared at all of us, her eyes piercing into our souls.

Isaac was frozen with terror as Delilah's knife got closer and closer to his throat. The knife brushed his neck, not piercing the skin, but it looked like it was freezing cold. "It was you…" I said, starting to cry again. "You killed Julia, didn't you?"

The others gasped, and Delilah just smiled.

"I knew it, you hell spawn! Damn you! I swear to God I'm gonna kill you! HOW DARE YOU KILL HER! DO YOU EVEN KNOW WHAT THAT DID TO US? TO GABRIEL AND I?!" I was both surprised and not surprised that she was the one who killed Julia.

I wished I could go over there and kill her for revenge, but Dimitri was holding me, keeping me from losing my mind.

"She was weak," Delilah scoffed, "she was literally stealing you from me. We were best

friends until she stole your time!"

"What the hell are you even talking about?" I was confused. Julia never "stole me as a friend." Maybe I was hanging out with her a little more than I do with Delilah, but that's no reason to kill her! Just talk to me about hanging out more! But even so, we're in a world war! Hanging out isn't really a priority anyway!

"You shouldn't be angry at me when you are being manipulated by the others, and if anything, you should be angry at yourself for allowing yourself to be controlled by them! Especially by Dimitri and Isaac after Julia was killed!" Delilah scowled, her knife getting even closer to Isaac, and his eyes widening even more as he fought back more intensely to free himself.

Isaac's flailing did nothing, sadly, and Delilah seemed bored, so she raised the knife to cut his throat open, but I held my hand out to stop her.

"Wait!" I screamed, hoping she wouldn't kill Isaac.

"What now?" Delilah shouted back, her glare spearing my heart and causing it to burn brighter than the fire.

The fire was actually starting to surround us and get closer every minute. "Please. Don't kill Isaac! He doesn't deserve to die. Not after we just got him back!" "You don't think I know that!? I was *wishing* he had died out here, but to my dismay, he survived."

Delilah glowered at his face, and the knife was lowered a little, but still near his neck in case anything was to happen.

We needed to move because the fire was starting to throw embers at our feet, so we started to move on the side, and Delilah was going to where we used to stand.

I'm not sure if Delilah would want to stand where we were, but I don't think she noticed.

With the source of the fire being behind Delilah now, it cast a shadow over her face, and her eyes began to glow ominously, which sent shivers down my spine.

"What will it take for you to release Isaac?" I begged, not really caring what she would say.

"That's simple. I want you to come with me into the fire!" Delilah cried, smiling to the point it was probably hurting her.

"Are you insane?!" I screamed, wishing she were joking.

"Oh, I am, probably…" she responded, giggling,

"But I don't care. I want us to die together.

Come and dance with me in hell, Livia! *It's the only way for Isaac not to die!*" Delilah started to die of laughter, and I began to consider her offer, but I looked at Dimitri, hoping he would understand.

"No," he stated, "I won't ever let you do that." "But it's the only way!" I pleaded.

"Maybe, but it doesn't mean you can't negotiate," Dimitri whispered.

"Delilah, please," I began, "can't there be anything else to make sure no one dies today?" "No. And now that I think of it, you have ten seconds to agree, or Isaac will die, and I'll come after you next!" Delilah's smile seemed to widen even more, which should be impossible. *No no no no no no no no no….* My mind was racing. I couldn't, but Isaac can't die!

I had no idea what I was supposed to do, and Gabriel was looking at me with grave eyes. Avery's eyes were full of worry and sadness. "Five seconds!" Delilah warned, still smiling intensely, and snickering under her breath, lifting the knife slowly back to Isaac's throat.

My eyes widened, and I knew I needed to make a decision, but I couldn't bring myself to speak.

Tears were rolling down my face like waterfalls, and my vision was getting more and more blurry, and I, as well as Dimitri and Gabriel, were starting to cough from breathing a little too much smoke.

"*TIMES UP!*" Delilah's smile faded, replaced with cold eyes and nothing else.

"*NO!*" I screamed, but it was too late, as Delilah slit Isaac's throat, and the red blood stained her face and hands.

I couldn't contain it anymore. I screamed as loud as I could possibly scream, to get it all out.

Time seemed to slow after that. The colors of the world, or lack thereof at this point, were fading away, but Delilah's eyes started to glow brighter and brighter, flickering both blue and red somehow.

Isaac's blood stayed the same as well, and the fire began to swallow his body, and Delilah was just standing, blase.

Delilah was still standing when the gun was fired, and the bullet pierced her heart, and as she fell, her face smiling, I was pulled away and was in someone's arms before I eventually passed out.

When I woke up, we continued running.

Ever since this war began, I've been running.

But now, I'm no longer running away on my own, though. I'm running with a new family in a messed-up hell of a world, going through yet another world war.